STRANGELY FIERCE FABLES

PAUL CARREO

For my family. My mother, sisters, brothers, nephews & most especially my father, William, who taught us the value of delightful absurdity and tall tales.

CONTENTS

FOREWORD

Welcome to the *First Edition* of my first published book. *(Holy smokes, I wrote a book this year!)*

It is my profound privilege to be able to share this collection of stories, from fantasy fiction to observational oddities, with the most treasured and supportive people in my life. *That's you!*

I have set a life mission to *lead & live through creative expression, embrace absurdity, and share joy*. And in this absurd year of 2023, I've spent my entire time doing just that! I chose to dedicate this year to becoming a better writer and artist because I believe that creative expression can make the world a better place. And I invite you in the year ahead to share in my strange tales, such that your imagination may also be stirred to shape a world of joy.

As for my self-deprecating disclaimer, setting the expectations bar to the floor: I have worked tirelessly to create a smooth and enjoyable reading experience with creative integrity. *But* I write and edit all this work as a one-man enterprise, so please be patient with the works that may still need a bit more polish in future editions. Your support and encouragement always helps me get there.

Please keep checking my website for new stories, essays, and artwork. And launching soon, follow my podcast on Spotify for all these stories as audiobooks.

Many thanks for reading and for sharing our joy together,

Paul Robert Carreo
www.paulcarreo.com

Strangely Fierce Fables:

*Fantasy fiction, literary shorts &
other absurdities*

Paul Carreo

INTRODUCTION

Imagination can shape the world, imbuing meaning to an otherwise meaningless and desolate spot in the galaxy. And absurdity, well, that's one of the most delicious forms of imagination, designed for a tickling jolt, reminding us the truth is never as serious as we like to pretend. Whether you are a fan of fantasy and speculative fiction or not, I've ensnared you here into my little arcade of strange fables and satirical tales. And lest you think you're in for an easy ride of fairy tales and life lessons, I warn you that some of these fables might bite you fiercely, in strange and unexpected places.

On behalf of my publishing company, PC Studios proudly presents **Strangely Fierce Fables**, a collection of such stories. It is broken into two books, plus some bonus essays. In the titular **Book One**, you will find my collection of fantasy fiction that range from folklore and ghost stories, to science-fiction and satire.

In **Book Two: Risings & Ramblings**, we shift to an observational style of literary shorts, which promise to dazzle you with my surreal filter over city life, travels and the modern world. You may have a natural preference for nonfiction prose over fables, and I encourage you to skip around to whatever grabs you. However, I hope you take the opportunity, as I did, to create some variance in your life views, exploring new appreciation for different genres.

Naturally, there is always something deeply vulnerable about sharing one's work. No doubt you may recognize me in many characters, no matter how outdated and ridiculous their ideals. But please do not dwell too deeply, for I believe many of the familiar served only for me to seed the parables and lore that have flourished beyond this mild mannered man.

We begin, as I did four years ago, with **A Coin for Lario's Sorrow**, my first conceived longform story. This novelette tells of the young man Lario, who pours all his troubles into a simple gold coin. His fate becomes quickly entangled with the fabled monster of the lake, who becomes cursed by the coin, and spreads her wraith on the quaint Italian laketown of Silica. I originally began this little legend on holiday in northern Italy, at my own little life crossroads, and learning about some of their local lore. I printed out a short booklet as a gift for my father that ended simply with emotional surrender and the 'monster' of neglect. That's what I needed it to be about then. And as I said earlier, life values move on, the story becomes bigger than the man, and the lessons take on new light. Presently, it's a heroic parable about friendship and empathy. But who knows what I'll need it to be about later.

Sisyphus Goes Job Hunting, is a reimagined Greek myth in the backdrop of the twenty-first century. You'll notice a lot of my stories, my creative bursts come during breaks between jobs, clearly a wonderful time for me to reflect. And this one is probably the most blatant of them all, in the aftermath of the 2020 lockdown. So blatant, I almost skipped writing a summary at all. But have a search for the Albert Camus essay, the Myth of Sisyphus, and perhaps you'll share my revelation that a tired immortal, pushing a boulder up a mountain, might actually have a smile on his face. *Many thanks to my good friend Ted Wiedenman for providing the playfully delightful artwork.*

The Haunting of Mr. Query, is a gothic flash fiction tale and a nod to my father's favorite way to scare his children before bed, *Edgar Allen Poe's The Raven*. I hope you appreciate the dense but meticulously chosen word choices and imagery. The little subversion of the horror genre at the end has divided my peers a bit. But consider, if you will, the relief of seeing the most horrid of monsters under your bed, in favor of dying a thousand deaths of trembling questions and dread. A special thanks to my friends at *Stoney's Writing Group* for prompting me with a one-word challenge, *'questions,'* during the Halloween season that led me here.

A Banshee's Bargain, an Irish ghost story, about a man who unwittingly makes a deal with the beautiful but duty-bound banshee that haunts the real-life Dublin pub, 'The Ferryman.' The meta wink here might evoke an image of me again, spending my years at 'The Ferryman,' an American born and Irish *naturalised* man, doing what the Irish ideal encourages. Sitting at a pub, sipping Guinness, reading Braham Stoker and Oscar Wilde, and waiting for the muses along the River Liffey to come knocking. I wrote a good bit of this tale from the basement cellar tavern of that pub on dark winter nights, warming myself with spirits, on my lips and in my mind.

Moving on to something lighter, the next two tales are speculative science-fiction with some whimsical irony. **Dead On Stats & Datasets**, is meant to be playfully paranoid, as you'd expect from a satirical look at life after death, or simulation, or wherever the heck you think we go next. This story started as a dare from my friend Greg, while hiking and laughing about the notion we might get a slide show presentation on our life at the 'pearly gates.' How refreshing it would be to see all your achievements up on a bar chart. On accepting the challenge, I naturally had to change St. Peter to a data engineer in a virtual simulator, as well as some influence from comedic icons like *Douglas Adams, Terry Prachet, & Neil Gaiman.*

New Phone, Who Dis? is an optimistic, although some have said a bit lonely, alien contact story. Writing this now in a time when everyone is divided on artificial intelligence and saturated with too much hyper-attention-demanding technology, I enjoyed imagining a near-future where we came out on the other side, a little bit calmer and cooler. Thanks to my friend Kieran, who's actually touched the original James Webb telescope, and got me interested in the potential of deep space observation. And thanks to my nephew Matthew for helping me ponder a nostalgic return to simpler tech and ways to connect. *(Sorry for roping you into this one, buddy, I owe you one).*

And just when you built your tolerance for the ridiculous and bizarre, I throw you **Prelude to Silverwater Tavern**. I stewed on this daft desert town of Silverwater, out of space and time, after having read a collection of stories dedicated to the 'weird western' genre from my father. I was hooked with possibilities of aliens, poltergeists and pirates caught up in a western bar, trading stories. This may feel absurd for many, unless you've spent any time imagining yourself at Star Wars' Mos Eisley cantina or riding inside the TARDIS of Doctor Who. And I really enjoyed pulling up a barstool and lingering with these odd bar denizens. I suspect there will be more stories to be poured in the future, as different patrons keep pulling up a stool to swill their tales.

Hermit and the Bear, is a flash fiction wilderness fable. Man versus beast versus wilderness is at its simplest and pointed here. I learned a nice lesson during this on writing concisely and feeling good about completing something end-to-end without overly fussing about the background.

Moving onto the second book, **Risings & Ramblings**, my observational and literary stories. I am always moved by authors who can create just as much surrealism as fantasy by telling stories 'based on true events.' Whether they're events already stranger than fiction, or a magnified inspection to find absurdity in the mundane, I love the opportunity to get in closer to things that might pass others by.

A Relegated Ship, Run Aground, a two part postmodern Dublin city tale. You could say this took me eleven years to write, watching with curious wonder, as the tides of the Irish economy have rushed in and out over decades past. This is a favorite amongst both my Irish and American friends, as it provides a deep history of modern events in Ireland that risk being forgotten. It aims to provide more empathy and understanding for the disenfranchised people in uncertain times. And it provides them with a fresh appreciation for the cycles of overreaching prosperity, collapse, and renewal - a petition, we as a people, should begin to look closer at and learn from our past. The featured Naomh Éanna ship is still standing in my neighborhood and several people, having read this, have mentioned their interest to campaign to save it from demolition. The featured houseless man Adam is based on someone I've been fascinated with for over a decade. Readers have also mentioned that homelessness in Ireland has been a fading issue that could use better awareness. Lastly, the character of Dublin stands proudly here trying to make sense of what to do in the decade ahead, as corporate buildings keep rising, along with foreign revenue and domestic debt. Still the good people of Dublin march proudly forward with a spirit of resilience.

'Book Two' continues with some lighter literary shorts. **Tiny Dormant Treasures**, was a piece I wrote last year, while visiting my mother, and digging around in the dirt in my recently passed father's garden. **A Frightful Fiend Doth Tread**, is based on a revelation I had several years ago, while traveling through the wild bush of East Africa. **Unleashed with Dogged Intent**, was something I had to pull out my laptop and write immediately when I saw this odd, leashless dog just trotting about outside a cafe, completely independent and self-assured. **A Captain's Compass North**, is a little parable of sorts, and I can't help thinking it's really just

one side of my brain lecturing the other. Still the backdrop of an iceberg breaking ship, exploring the north Artic pass, makes me want to be there under the Aurora Borealis.

Both **Irish Fleets Wave Good Luck** and **Entangled States with an Irish Addict** represent that time on lockdown when so many of us shared a sense of total isolation collectively. I've read many new stories bubbling up more and more now, in the aftermath of the pandemic. And I'm happy to find that any type of trauma people have faced in those unique years, big or small, we have spent the time giving grace through self-reflection. And **The Matrix of Living Abroad**, well, I couldn't help myself here. A reflection on the strange surrealism a big fish like me can often feel, so far from his home pond.

Epilogues & Reflections is where I added some bonus works and personal essays. I'll highlight **The Octagon**, as the first creative writing I can recall as an adult, without any agenda and for its own sake. Still today, it rattles my soul and notions of manifest destiny, reading the eerily familiar perils I wrestled with, still so pertinent to me, *nineteen years later*. Finally have a look at the comic retellings of some sick Carreo family pranks, which might give you a glimpse into why I am, well, the way I am. As this whole tomb provides, I hope you get a closer look at my imagination, as well as spark a burning flame in your own.

Book I: Strangely Fierce Fables, *the fantasy fiction*

A Coin for Lario's Sorrow

A Coin for Lario's Sorrow

*A creature fable
by Paul Carreo*

A Coin for Lario's Sorrow, *a creature fable*

"... no point worrying about that problem, our ole lake monster, she's already busy chewing on that particular coin..."

Part I: Lariosauro, just an old lake monster

Deep in the belly of an Italian lake, lived an old lumbering beast from the ancient world. The lake was named Lario, meaning deep and reflecting, and had been sculpted by colossal glaciers eons ago. This lake aptly boasted the deepest and most shimmering waters across all the surrounding Alps. The old beast sometimes wondered if she came to live in this lake because of its depths or if it was deep because she lived there. Nonetheless the creature, despite being quite colossal, bigger than most whales in fact, found her home to be quite capacious and cozy indeed.

She had never actually seen a whale, incidentally, but had gleaned these things from the whispered stories of the many shoals of chatty delicious fish. Oh those delicious schools of plentiful lake fish. Most would fill her large belly without complaint but sometimes bartered their lives for stories of the outside world. The lake beast delighted in hearing about open oceans and these friendly blubbering whales, even when it all felt so impossibly big and fantastic. Like the many wonders beyond the lake's borders, there were so many mysteries hiding in the corners of her old mind. She had trouble recalling how long she had been living in this mountain enclosed lake. To her it was some place she had always been. To her, it was a timeless haven, an intrinsic part of her being, a story in itself.

And it was a good story too, one she retold every day with gratitude, as she spent the long days in her own perfect paradise. Indeed she learned the value of sharing stories, and they seemed to quench her desire to be anywhere else. Many tales were woven by her seafood companions, who bubbled giddily but often misremembered the details of their days. And then there were the tales she overheard from those clever shirt-wearing apes who walked upright along the shoreline. They painted worlds more intricate than eyes or ears could every capture and she liked those best of all.

For nearly two hundred years she watched these strange wobbly leg-walkers make fire, make war, make love, and make up some of the most wonderfully tall tales. She found herself often hiding in the depths, spying on their strangely animated ways. And on warm summer evenings, when her sister Moon was still asleep low beyond the mountain ridge, she would linger longer by the shoreline campfires to hear these busy critters chatter away.

The hairless, shirted apes would spend hours jabbering their mouth flaps at each other, assisted by exaggerated hand gestures. She would often look at her own short fins and wave them about in silly mimicry, before feeling self-conscious and giving up entirely. She would even blow bubbles in hopes that they would burst at the surface into similar sounding musical words. This often ended with disappointed, but wise, abandonment of such monkey business.

A few times through the seasons she had been careless in her eavesdropping and was spotted by these shirt-wearing mouth flappers. They would point and crowd around the shore, in what she deemed a large overreaction. And the lake would grow turbulent with boats for weeks on end, causing many seasons of unnecessary disruption to her peaceful fishing. Times like these quickly taught her to be more private as she bided her time in deeper hidden chasms. She understood how overexcited these wobbly hand-wavers tend to get, and decided it was best they stayed friends from afar.

Little did she know for all this fuss over her sightings, one positive thing had emerged from the upright apes. They began to steadily repeat the same words in her presence, and it became clear that they were trying to give her a name. They called her things like 'lake monster', 'dinosaur' and 'reptile'. They even compared her to the story about a possible cousin named Nessie from a land far up north. They quibbled about the right words to use and some even used smarter sounding names like Ples-ee-o-saur. But eventually they settled on naming her after their own lake and took to calling her 'Lariosauro.'

Well, she had never met this cousin beast they whispered about, although she was sure jealous of how cute her name rolled off the tongue. Still, she had never had a name before and she supposed *'Lariosauro'* was a delightfully round sounding one. So she accepted the gift gleefully and adored it like a jewel. She didn't know much about the ways of these silly apes, but she sure loved the way they made sense of things with names. But whenever she felt overwhelmed with their wild imaginations and made-up problems, she would make a fast dive to easily solve the only one that troubled her, a hungry belly.

On a particularly beautiful day, the majestic and newly named Lariosauro was happily on the hunt to fill herself with the bounties of this vast paradise. After having her fill, she tried prodding these fish for any new stories from afar but quickly grew weary from their same old misremembered tales. And just then, she saw reflecting on the water's edge, an unfamiliar and peculiar upright ape, slowing his shoreline steps, gazing full of woe into the abyss, and weaving a new story that filled her with a captivating sorrow.

Part II: Lario, just another peculiar upright ape

This woefully peculiar ape was among a tribe of lakefolk who called themselves villagers. Like the Lariosauro, this upright walking primate was enjoying his solitude in the serenity of the open waters and its twinkling reflections. Unlike the old lake monster, he seemed to be muttering his lonely heart's song aloud, and showed no delight in the bounties of fish or the whispers of their stories.

The young man's name was Lario, also named after the lake where he was born, aptly sharing its qualities of depth and reflection. He had spent his entire life, along these lakefront shores, in the medieval relic port town named Silica. Lario had never traveled beyond the barriers of the

Alps, but often retreated from the bustle of Silica's townsquare to the neighboring monastic villas, who boasted the most vibrant botanical gardens in all the land. Today was such a day of retreat from his troubles, as Lario walked mindfully along a sandy path of hanging blossoms and waving cypress trees.

Lario wore his heavy heart, pondering the great toils of his labors, losses of the past, and the dread of an uncertain tomorrow. It was, afterall, his namesake and burden to ponder such trivial worries. He told himself little stories about what kind of man he wished to be and what kept him from those wishes. He thought little about the history of the world, the great legends and heroes of the past, and even the myths and lore surrounding this lake. He had no time for silly stories of forefathers and forebodings, wagging their fingers at him. And least of all, he had no time for stories of romantic tales and lake monsters from the deep.

Stuck in his own head, Lario strode along the Sunday shores this one fine day. He had suffered the loss of a good friend and grew more and more vexed every day about his own death. His nights had grown sleepless. His work days had grown sedated. And his free time, well, it was spent overthinking his own purpose. Stuck in a rut of his own discontent. Even this lovely Sunday, striding along the glory of a late summer beach, all he could ponder was the work week ahead.

Through his mourning, he was filled with self-pity and resented his gossipy coworkers at the local bank. His need for peace over riches and titles was never understood by his wicked, scheming boss. And his once happy days toiling away at a clerk's desk, waned to a lonely despair with many hours staring out his tiny window.

All of these collected sorrows of the week were stewing and settling thicker than usual inside his mucky head. And true to Lario's habits of reflection on these weekend strolls, these thoughts began swirling their way into a particularly rank story he loved to repeat:

"I am unique but I am alone. I have struggles beyond what anyone could understand. I work harder than most to overcome them. More than I should. I am under-appreciated and conspired against. The world is against me. I am unable to rescue myself. I don't feel safe and protected like when I was a child. And perhaps, just maybe, I am my own worst enemy."

Lario continued to mutter this curse upon himself, plodding through the majestically lush gardens. Despite the gray clouds in his mind, the sun seemed to beg for his attention with dancing prismic colors, as a calm warm breeze rocked the magnolia trees. Lario was helpless to defy the beauty of the present moment any longer, and felt jolted out of his own head with a marveling gasp. And so, by the grace of the day, he found himself no longer able to focus on his sorrow. His senses were overloaded by the soothing sways of triumphant pines and the perfumery of plump citrus fruit.

In this moment, this disquieted young man found a certain peace in putting his old stories aside. He leaned over and rested his arms across a stone carved railing, wondering what it would feel like to stuff these stories in a sack and toss it into the lake forever. This rare revelation inflamed his imagination and he was suddenly enveloped by the warmth of this new idea.

"This could be the answer! I don't need to be clutching so deliberately to my problems, after all. They haven't served me, they've only made me unhappy. I could just leave them all behind. Right here, right now! Drop them off my shoulders at this spot at the lake. And walk away forever!" Lario exclaimed exhilarated across the open water. *"No more resisting them or debating them. Give them no more attention... and decide to let go."*

Enraptured by this choice, Lario was momentarily interrupted by the horn of the last running ferry for the day. It billowed smoky diesel engines from afar and beckoned its sunset passengers to board. He became alert from his dreamy state, and rifled through his pockets for enough coinage to make the trip home. Glancing down at his handful of gold coins, he was tempted to replay his worries for money, the one that robbed him of faith in his own ability. The story that reminded him how he gave his dignity to his job in exchange for these coins. And in that story he felt the old fear, guilt, and sin that sent him along this road in the first place.

"Right, no more!" the young man realized, "I'll pack away my sorrows and leave them at the bottom of this lake forever. But what to pack them in? A mere ruck sack would never do. No, a cloth bag would never survive the decay of time. Nor would the strongest rope remain untattered in the endless tides. No, no, it would have to be something stronger. A symbol capable of capturing the imagination and ideals of man. A promise. A coin."

He looked down into his open palm and from the pile of change, and a few buttons, he plucked from the top a single gold coin, minted and full of promise. It was perfect. Forged by man to last the ages and endowed with the shared beliefs of an entire civilization. This coin was meant to house some powerful magic. So into it he poured his sorrow, casting a spell that imbued it forever with his cursed stories. And standing over his wishing well, he gave it one last kiss goodbye and hurled the coin far away in exile seemingly for all of time.

Lario watched the small treasure shimmer brightly, as it skipped wildly across the lake's surface, before plunging to the inevitable depths. And just as he began to turn for his ferry, he caught a glimpse at a mirage that made him rub his eyes. Through blinding sunset refractions, a slick gray marbled head broke the surface, opened wide jaws, and its arched back looped into a diving pursuit of that heavy gilded lure.

Lario paused in disbelief. But with his soul now free of stories and speculations, he found only the need to return a small chuckle. He bounced off to his ferry, skipping with a lighter heart, feeling the beginnings of a renewed vow, a promise of freedom from his darkest of days. Or so it seemed.

Part III: A lost coin and the brightest of days

All the ride home, this young man Lario, felt graced by something invisible that had no name or no known story. Something that simply existed for his protection. His *dread* of the week ahead had evaporated because his mind had been freed from the confines of all those niggling 'what ifs.'

"What if I can't, what if I'm wrong, what if it's hard, what if I fail, what if I'm mocked"?

None of these questions mattered anymore because he knew all the previous 'what ifs' in his life had never truly protected him. Not the way he felt now.

He felt no more *guilt* because he no longer felt bound by judgment. No judgment from others nor from himself. He felt no more *sin*, for sin was only another word for disconnection. Disconnection from yourself, your purpose, your present moment of being. And his connection towards a new purpose could not have felt stronger.

Standing off the bow of the ferry, wind whipping through his black locked hair, Lario looked across the waters of his namesake, staying free of old doubts and reservations. The only story he felt compelled to ponder at all, as he glanced portside, was the very real possibility that a very unreal creature had just swallowed his terrible gold coin whole. He knew the folklore of the Lariosauro, although until now, had never considered their entwined names. He recalled the campfire tales brought to life so well by his father, who loved to frighten and tease. He remembered the big photo hoax many summers passed, so clearly forged to vaguely show the beast's silhouette. And so obviously staged to bring large waves of tourists into the town.

And now, if only for his father's sake, he decided to tell himself a big fish story. He decided to believe in the Lariosauro. She existed because he needed her to exist. He needed to believe that someone would be chewing on that cursed coin for him. And he thought, maybe all beasts, all faeries, all gods and monsters, heaven and hell, live in that space between faith and need.

As the ferry came to the port of Silica, Lario stepped into the dawn of his new days, blissful but admittedly naive. Naive to the poison he had unwittingly left behind for that poor gentle beast. Regardless, he walked the town with a fresh cloak of confidence, befuddling townsfolk, who had only known Lario as the town worrywort. He stopped first at the local bar, the Cafe Onice Nero (which meant Black Onyx, but he never knew why). He quickly found it unbearable to listen to the pub dweller's onslaught of woes and self-pity.

Still Lario would return many times to interrupt their misery with his new favorite story of the lake creature, who was there to swallow up all their problems. He gave them all his full assurance their problems were no longer necessary because they now belonged to something else. Something strong enough to hold them. Something in the deep, busying herself with those niggles on their behalf.

"Now there, no point worrying about that. Our ole lake monster, she'll be busy chewing on that particular coin for you." He would say, with a calm hand on his neighbor's shoulder. Or, *"Oh dear, that's a shame, the poor Lariosauro is probably choking on that rough coin."* Or, *"I'd bet that old Lariosauro's belly is aching fiercely on that rotten coin."* And when it seemed a trivial enough problem indeed, *"Leave it alone, the Lariosauro is probably about ready to pass that old coin."*

The town denizens would laugh at Lario's carefree nature and flippant replies. Often taking comfort for a while, that their burdens were not real. Worries of money, worries for their children, worries of death, worries for tomorrow. And always, Lario would retort,

"...oh, that's a tough one, but don't worry, you can bet that clever Lariosauro is picking his teeth clean with that jagged coin for you."

Lario went through his days with this lightness, carefree to everyone in town and at his gloomy job at the bank. Sometimes his indifference would betray him, like when his duties at the bank gave way to missed deadlines. Or when his confidence was mistaken for cold callousness to the troubles of others. But he never wavered in his new promise for total freedom.

Lario would spend the many seasons ahead in his dizzy joy, renewing his oath each night by the moonlit lake. He swore wouldn't act so foolishly as to see the shiny allure of worry, and take that bait, like the downtrodden townsfolk do each day. Or like that poor lumbering lake monster did on that one fateful day.

Part IV: A coin's curse and paradise lost

Deep in the belly of an Italian lake, through dark and troubled waters, stirred a monster from the ancient world. Many moons had passed since that fateful day of her curse. Lariosauro's belly was haunted and tormented with the personal demons of a man she did not know. Now she howled feverishly each and every night, chasing away the birds and the fish in terror.

Her body glowed hot from that fiery coin, turning her skin to green dragon scales, Her stomach rumbled spitefully as her agony sizzled. She could not think of anything that used to give her joy. Not fish, not stories, not even her friends Night Sky and Moon, who seemed so cold and distant behind dark clouds. Her blood boiled with contempt for the trivial ways of man, as she forgot the delights of her once perfect paradise. She thought only of the man's discarded coin, his abandoned turmoil that became her own.

So the Lariosauro became what she always was to these men, a monster. She began to boil the lake water to steam and into a slow rising fog. That fog grew thicker and thicker with every unseen and turning moon. Until one day, it grew into shadows and crept wraith-like in the night to the towns of men, in search of sad souls to possess and spread torment.

The fog wraiths looked long and low for the man named Lario to return his spell but to no avail, he could not be found. In the deep, the monster continued to spew her venom upon the surrounding valleys. She cursed the many over the few, one evening at a time. For it was not one man's sorrow that Lario had been carrying that fateful day. But the stories and greed of the entire town of Silica.

This lake monster swore she would share her agony, as she reigned down chaos to those so sure of their protected happy lives. Her rage poisoned the air with hot breath, bringing early winters, and blotting the sun. Her vengeance swift, she withered the lands and overfished the waters, spitting out the spoils along the seashore to rot.

And when that didn't satiate her need for torment, she would reveal herself in all her magnificent horror to a lonely sailor. In a violent battery, her whipping tail would bash their hulls to splinters. And the desolate few who survived would tell their tales to others in vain to a disbelieving unsympathetic lot.

Such was the fate of the old ferryman, Captain Charn, who struggled to make his business running from port to port. He ran the same ferry that Lario was riding home on the day the coin's curse was first cast. The Lariosauro had since made her den at the cove by the old botanic gardens, far from the main town. Chewing up fish heads, bringing in scavenging birds and spreading a dank blight that plagued the lands. She laid plunder to Captain Charn one day, capsizing the old ferry, and nearly leaving him for dead. But the skipper rode his boat upside down and adrift to safety, a sole survivor left to tell his impossible tale.

Now decommissioned and dividing his days between ship repairs and the local cafe, he would often drink too much beer and weave his insane stories of the encounter with this dark creature. He told the weary troubled pubfolk, who were drowning their sorrows in more local news, about the forgotten port that was no longer traveled. And he warned the people of SIlica of the surrounding blight, from the monster that let him live, only to be dismissed as a madman.

And so the town grew darker each day and the monster in the depths unrelentingly bellowed a tune of vengeance, a new song she sang, a new story she would write herself, the story of one man's sorrow and another's wrath.

Part V: Two sides of the same coin

So for the next decade Silica and the neighboring villages fell into a dark curse of shadow and fog. The winter season lingered frigid and longer each year. With the colder nights and looming mist, the townsfolk found themselves huddling indoors from nature's wickedness. Crowded into the Onice Nero each night, they exchanged tales of scandal that now crept so easily into their dark imaginations.

Although they never believed the tall tales of Captain Charn, they grew more suspicious of black magic coming from the tall Alps across the lake and its surrounding dark forest. They stopped going for walks along the grim seashore, for distaste of the nasty winds and dark fog. They took no pride in their harvests and their fishing hauls became slim. They drank wine to soothe their woes and grew fat in wasted grief.

Some of the villagers still prospered in their greedy, ambitious pursuits.

But they were only counting their money to bury the guilt for the backs they built their houses on. Other villagers found solace in these dark days by resigning themselves with hunched backs to soulless duty and hard labor. But they were only busying their hands to forget their troubles at home.

The villagers told stories of angry gods and mountain demons, in whispered voices around stone hearths. They felt sure they were being punished and felt ashamed for sins unknown. The entire town bickered fiercely in scorn of each other. They pointed fingers, suspicious of the wrongdoings of others, casting blame and creating new names for people. Names like blasphemer, infidel, & witch. Lynchmobs would swell up to capture anyone they named as a wrongdoer, suspected to commune with the devil himself. Anyone they could blame and cast away for their troubles.

Somewhere lost between the town's divided attention from madness to apathy, there was Lario. Walking on cloud tops and keeping a distance from the gossip. Bounding from task to task, day to day, season to season. Light as a whisper and seemingly at peace. It had been two winters now living this way, fully detached from worry and wary of those who tried to peddle tales of self-pity.

The bank had given up trying to work him any harder. In his content, Lario could no longer be bothered showing any desire for further responsibility. As he was prone to remind his coworkers, he had everything he needed. He would remind them often of his coined expression of a simple lake monster, minding his fussings for him. Lario found himself leaving his day's work earlier and earlier to spend time in his tiny garden, away from all the fussy business of more eager men.

And although he felt unburdened by the worries of the town, he couldn't help feeling the more he withdrew from these dark days, the worse the town was getting. There was a contempt brewing thicker and Lario began peeking out from his blissful curtains to wonder why.

His curiosities eventually lead him back to the town's waterhole. And as much as he loathed hearing people's elbow-to-elbow complaints, he still longed for the company and tolerated their small town gossip for a time. Lario would bounce from one table to another each night, never much interested in the scandal and dismissive of what sounded more and more like naive nostalgia for better days.

Two of the older fishermen pulled up chairs to trade such complaints about their hauls, saying that each year the bounty got smaller, and it seemed all the fish had just packed up and moved to cleaner waters. Lake Lario, not the man, was in fact getting murkier by the season. And an invasive algae seemed to be crawling out to eat away at their docks.

"It's no wonder we have no tourists or money coming in, even in the summer months. The sun's never out past this blasted fog, our lake smells like rotten eggs, and our docks are all falling apart." The old man shook their heavy heads, hoisting heavier pints.

"Have you heard? Just last week those teenage hooligans burnt the southwest docks to the ground, out of spite or boredom, who knows," sputtered a man from the next table. "These kids were turning into a pack of wolves. They can't get jobs, they have nowhere to go, no money to get there if they did. And the more the town falls into spoil, the easier it is for them to piss all over it."

"Exactly, just ask the florist or the old toy maker, they've had everything from bricks to flaming bottles launched through their storefront windows. What do you make of all this Lario, dare I even ask?" The gritty patrons would turn briefly from their pint glasses, testing to see if he even cared at all.

"I think, fellas, you can turn all these worries over to the old Lariosauro monster. Just don't you go boiling your own stomach over it. All will be well again. Someday." Lario smiled a little with his attempted reassurance.

But the cafe dwellers found no solace in his tired expressions and silly parables. They didn't want to hear about mythical beasts in their commiseration. So they waved Lario off and changed tables for more sympathetic company. Folks who didn't talk in fairytales and shared their sense of dread.

Shouting from the far corner of the bar, cried Captain Charn, who had quickly gained the reputation as the town drunk. He walked into the middle of the room waving his ale around.

"Lario's more right than he knows! I would be listening to him about that old lake dragon. She's holed up near Raven's Cove, where the old monastery was, I've seen her with my own two eyes! That's where all the dead fish are washing up. Where the murky water is as thick as oil. That's the den of Lario's old lake monster, I tell you. I know, because that's where she throttled my old poor ferry."

"Raven's Cove? It's not called that, you mean Villa Monastero? As for the Lariosauro… rubbish, I say. A nursery rhyme. Just a legend to get tourists coming back!" The younger patrons started booing and cackling at the unhinged captain to sit back down. Most just turned their backs, dismissing the old barnacle. Others joined in to bully him further, pulling him into their circles and egging him on.

"You've seen her then, have you? Tell us *all* about her. This giant dragon, you say, in our lake. How come we've never seen her?" They prodded and poked, as more of the young lads joined in for the thrashing.

"Oh she's real, all right. I swear my merchant's pension on it. Damn monster put me out of business. It was only last winter when I decided to go check in on that withered old garden village that pulled in all our tourists. Imagine my surprise that cold dark night, when I rounded the lake's bend to see the once beautiful cove rotting and polluted. Dead fish floating everywhere, nasty black crows and scattered crabs, going mad with bloodlust. All pecking away at each other like asylum inmates. And the stench was so thick that my sails got soaked and weighed down" The young drunkards kept rounding him and throwing peanuts, but Captain Charn continued undeterred, mistaking this for encouragement.

"So there I was, stuck in the dank of the Raven's Cove, crows swarming around like aphids. I just stood there aghast, dead winded or run aground in the filth, I couldn't tell which. I began fretting fiercely as to how I was going to wade my way out and get back to open water. In my fussing about, I heard her deep guttural bellow. It was the beast and I felt strangely like it was responding to my worries. She rose slowly from the water, a demon leviathan, she was." He got somber and the crowd hushed but for a few snorts.

"She hoisted her slick green snake head high over my bow. She hissed at me through her sharp teeth, before her jaws opened wide and came crashing down through my foredeck. I was capsized, but at least it knocked me out of the muck. So I grabbed the bottom rudder and began paddling furiously away. She didn't seem to want to follow, but here look, I still got splinters all stuck in my leg to prove it." He threw his filthy leg up on the bar and started to reveal the crusty scars, as the crowd booed him with disgust.

At this, the barkeep had had enough. And he finally interrupted the show to throw the old drunk out by the collar. Lario seemed the only one in the cafe not chuckling. Lost in a retrieving memory, he was about to take another swing of his ale when he noticed the neighboring table all staring at him expectedly.

"Well, Lario? Do you know anything about what that lunatic is saying? Have you been feeding him your ridiculous stories about that monster? I know your father was a fan of a big fish tale. Tell me you don't *really* believe in that old bedtime story."

"You know old gents, I can't say what that old fool saw or claims to have seen. But a good story is only as good as how useful it is in your life. So if there is a lake monster, well, maybe she could serve you some good too. Just as she has for me. I've been sitting here trying hard to listen to all your doom and gloom stories. But I mean what I've told you before. You would be better off just casting it all out into the lake."

And with that Lario took his leave again, shrugging off these small town problems, and leaving the patrons to shake their heads, befuddled at the riddles of this callous young man.

Little did anyone expect and least of all Lario, these laketown legends would prove very real indeed. And as the townsfolk of Silica continued to fill themselves with the dread of the worst things to come, busying themselves with whispers and gossip, the lake kept boiling all their worries into steam. The monster in the lagoon was growing more alive and vengeful with every dark thought they fed her.

The Lariosauro was no longer just chewing over the coin of sorrow she had first swallowed. She was not just picking her teeth with it in ponderance. Over the seasons, that gold coin burned hot from the burdens of others, and she was closing in on her weighty appetite for chaos and revenge.

For indeed, one man's sorrow is another one's wrath. They are two sides of the same coin. It wasn't Lario's fault for unwittingly tossing his troubles aside like a snowball down a mountain. But the very next day, it

became clear, as the night sky used to be, that his soul, his fate, and the fate of the whole town - were all entwined with the very real monster of his own making.

Part VI: Silica, the turning stone

The people of Silica were suffering and their joy was gone. And yet, there were still some folk who remained resilient in these times of shadow and fog. They continued to huddle together, commiserating and trading empathy in their times of loss. Listening quietly to each other, while sharing modest meals and warm drinks. This was the true spirit of Silica. And so they gathered every night at the Onice Nero, finding new ways to name their pain and support each other.

The next evening after the bullying of the poor old Captain Charn, Lario returned to the cafe, a bit hat in hand, to find a sight for sore eyes. Around a center table were three old men, scattered empty pint glasses, more glasses than elbow room, and his only true remaining friend, Santino. The men blathered on about their troubles, as expected, speculating on a bad growing season ahead, while the bank was on a rampage for foreclosures.

Santino, whose name meant *'little saint'*, was wiser than his years suggested. He sat there silently listening, his kind patient eyes glimmering with respect for his elders. He was always like this, rarely interrupting except to offer encouragement. Santino didn't need to speak at all some nights, only to demonstrate he was there listening. And the people would open their hearts to him uninhibitedly. He was the town's philosopher in many ways and Lario would be lost without him.

"Lario knows what I'm talking about." The cries and attention came from the ferryman in the back corner, retelling the same story as the night before. And as before, he started bragging about the splinter scars on his leg. And once again, before he could show off the signs of his run-in with the Lariosauro, the barkeep took over the story and threw him back out by the collar. This time, the small mob was so wound up they happily followed him out into the street to continue the night's heckling. And with half of the loud drunk bar missing, things grew a bit quieter.

The folks around Lario's table, Santino included, sunk into whispered tones and tried again to bring Lario back into the fold. "Can't seem to get away from that tall tale you're always spewing on about. You going mad like the ferryman, or what?" a red bearded man said, quivering his voice and hands for dramatic effect. "Hold any water or just some bullshit you like to spill to keep away from all the troubles?" The stout man looked him dead in the eye, not really expecting much back from Lario.

There was a long silence and Lario scanned around the averted eyes, on the wrong end of an inside joke at his expense. One old man even spit on the floor, and muttered 'coward' under his breath. They all seemed to nod knowingly at each other like they had all already decided everything they needed to know about him.

Finally, Santino broke the silence and stood up suggesting that he and Lario take a walk outside to get some fresh air from the stale stares. Lario gladly accepted, retreating from the scowls on his back. Once outside, standing between cold empty patio tables, Santino put his hand on Lario's shoulder.

"Trust me, that was for your own good, you were about to suffer the same fate as the poor mad ferryman. And I tell you, Lario, you seem to be heading that direction more and more. I just wanted to ask, what's become of you? You used to be so well respected here. You used to make us laugh. You used to drink and linger longer."

Lario started to explain how badly he had collapsed under his own weight. And how badly he needed to believe that his sorrows had been cast off forever. But he stalled and let Santino continue.

"Look, you know I respect you. I really do. I too often wonder if this whole town of Silica isn't spending too much time drowning their sorrows and not enough time doing anything about it. We seem to have dark times when we dwell on dark times. We seem to have warm summers when we tell ourselves happy tales. But you, you seem to show no care in either season. It's like I've lost my friend to some, I don't know, ghost."

Larios blinked and stood still before shaking off the question. "Maybe, but at least I'm a free ghost. Free from all this moping about. I tried to listen to this gossip, Santino, I really did. You're my friend, and I have missed you too. I just realized that I had a choice to make. A choice on which things to give a damn about. And just like magic, I realized the things that hurt me were also my choice to leave behind."

"Don't get me wrong, I try to care about the troubles in town, I really do. It's just that most of the time, it all feels so trivial and not worth gnawing on. I feel better knowing that most of my worries are sitting at the bottom of..." Lario was interrupted by his friend.

"Right at the bottom of the lake, getting gnawed on by some dragon. Yeah, I know the tale, you've said it a hundred times. But listen now, Lario, this monster you've revived, this old legend, I sort of understand it. You need to believe in it, it serves a purpose for you. You need to know something else is minding the problems that plagued you for too long. And that coin you always talk about, well that was your turnstone."

"A turnstone? Yes, exactly, a conductor." Lario added. "Just like the town of Silica. Did you know this whole town was built on a quartz mountain, speaking of a turning stone? And did you ever notice this whole place changes color like a mood ring? The sun was shining once, and we're all so smug about it like we invented sunshine and it will last forever. We face a few hard times, and look at us, all your so-called friends turn on each other. They gossip, they scramble to cut each down. They get dark and lose themselves to dark whispers. Is that what you want me to return to? I barely understand why a good man like you can tolerate them all."

"It's because they're my tribe, Lario! I love them for all their faults, not despite them." Santino leaned in for one last attempt to intervene, "Look, I love you, I really do. But I fear you've lost something when you threw that coin away. A piece of your soul or something, I don't know."

"So what choice do you want me to make? You want me to sit here and listen each night to all the doom and gloom, the cancer of complaints? It's not helping your soul either, Santino. How can you stand it?"

"Well it's not always as bad as you say." Santino wandered into the brick road, marveling up at a full pink moon, peaking rarely through parting clouds. "Sometimes I just need to unwind over a beer. Sometimes I need to remind myself my niggles aren't so bad. Often I just like listening to the woes, because I know they're never as terrible as they sound. But the people need to get them out of their guts to move on."

Lario continues to fold his arms, shaking his head unconvinced. "I don't know if I agree. Worry only begets worry. And the town is only plagued because they are winding each other up with their own sins. Hubris, envy, gossip. That's all I hear. Hubris and envy gripped us even when the sun was out, like the roosters at the bank, all taking credit for the dawn. But gossip is the worst sin, it's the one that leads to contempt. Which is where we all seem to be now. Hubris and envy are like campfires, they can be contained. But gossip and collusion are buckets of kerosene on that fire. They're the dark whispers that turn into forest fires. And we do it every night here."

"My friend, listen to me closely. You are truly lost if you believe that." Santino came in close to Lario now, with kind eyes but stern words. "What you call collusion, I call camaraderie. We have gotten through these dark times not in spite of our comforting whispers, but because of them. It is my belief, and I hope you will see this someday, that the burdens of life cannot be carried alone. Friends are there to share each other's burdens. Some of them are less serious than others, sure, but they're still there to trade and bond over. Show patience with them and you'll hear them for what they are.

'When am I going to make time to mend my fence? How will I make my mortgage this month? How can I reconnect with my wife? Will my daughter ever marry?' These things I chew on with my friends so they don't fester in my gut for long. Do you understand?"

Lario thought about it for a bit, but again started to retreat into his familiar armor. "And those are all very interesting things to chew on, I'm sure, to occupy your time. But I tell you you're wasting your time, because that old Lariosauro, she's…"

"… I know, I know, that old Lariosauro should be picking her teeth clean, chewing on those problems for me." Santino smiled a little with resignation and let it go.

"Exactly." Lario chuckled a bit as he tightened his coat, and kept walking home under the low street lamps of the cobbled streets of Silica. His friend Santino, stayed closely by his side, hopeful that Lario would spend the cold silent moment between them pondering his advice.

Although he didn't say it outloud, it was truly the most sincere invitation to change Lario had heard in years. An invitation let go of this axe he seemed to be grinding for the troubles of others. An invitation to lose this chip on his shoulder, that he thought he had cast away. And it came from the only person that he trusted more than himself. A friend that accepted him no matter what.

Part VII: Reclaiming one's coin

Santino continued to walk Lario home, both clutching their coats against the cold misty night. Lario felt a strange calm in the silence, gripped with old niggles he hadn't felt in a while. Familiar feelings of shame and despair that had been there all along. Feelings he suspected that even his coin couldn't hold, nor the lake monster would be willing to chew for him. And yet he didn't seem to mind them as much. He felt comfort in knowing he had his friend by his side again.

As they rounded the corner away from the cafe, the two stopped dead in their tracks to find a horrific sight they could barely believe. A bright orange glowed a hot inferno all around the town's bank, roaring and aflame. Smoke was billowing out busted windows, as a small gang gathered and cackled on the sidewalk, cheering the building to burn to the ground. A few of them turned around when they sensed Lario and Santino, eyes fading from impish pride to hostility. Lario was sickened by the scene and without thinking jumped in scornfully, grabbing a flaming bottle out of one of the young lad's hands. Santino tugged Lario's arm to retreat, knowing how quickly this could turn ugly, as the whole gang began to circle them.

But it was too late for a fast escape. Around the corner came the howling of Captain Charn, still being chased and bullied by the drunk pub folk from earlier. The pursuing lynch mob screeched to a halt in front of the spitting fire, shifting aghast gazes between the younger hooligans and Lario, who was still holding the confiscated bottle bomb. The bank's marauders took this opportunity to shift the blame, pointing their fingers, "Lario's burning down his bank, we knew he was up to no good, we caught him in the act, look!"

The village ferryman never broke his stride, still hightailing it down a path to the lake. And rather than trying to explain the situation, Santino took this as a cue to follow, grabbing Lario by the collar and fleeing together. The two mobs quickly joined forces and pursued the three men, picking up sticks and lighting torches from the hot inferno. But the ferryman was clever, jumping over the side of a footbridge into a small stream of sewer runoff. Lario and Santino followed reluctantly, as the mob plundered past, confused and angry. As the three conferred on a plan, Captain Charn led them, swimming quietly to the lake to the newly repaired steamship he had moored. He promised to sail to the safer harbor of Lario's home port across the lake. And so the two men followed.

Before long, the steam engine started pumping black plumes, and the ferryman was secretly pleased to be hosting two passengers again. Off in the distance were the orange orb torchlights of the mob, searching like angry glowworms along the coastal road. Lario knew immediately they would be heading to his home, perhaps even waiting for him by the time this old boat got there. He looked at the captain, whose frenzied eyes had settled themselves back to those of a confident seafarer.

The old ferryman was moving with purpose again, deftly finding his bearings, downshifting his engines and hoisting the outfitted sails. With Santino's help, they cut a tight jib, beating windward on a calm night. It was safer and quieter this way. And perhaps something about the breeze in skipper's hair reminded Lario that they had both been men of dignity in better days. Lario began to think again about the ferryman's raving story, so easily spat at, so easily dismissed at the cafe, and now jogging his own buried memory of an impossible day.

The ferryman believed in Lario's lake monster, more than Lario did himself. The spotting of that mythical creature, on that one miracle day, had faded so much into fable, that he never even bothered to consider it could be real. So as the course smoothed out, Lario asked him more about what he knew and quickly discerned that it was the same cove where he had made his wish. According to the old captain, the monster had been busy there making its filthy den. Mangey black ravens swarmed along the beach, hence the nickname Raven's Cove. With the thick smell of rot in the air, the gardens had withered to wastelands.

What followed was much worse, a disease of skin rot spread among the locals, and scared off any hope of neighboring support. No person was well enough to leave town, all cowarded in their own illness in boarded up houses, fearful of looters. The docks fell quickly into shambles, making it impossible for any vessel to make port. No one traveled to see the gardens, no ship came in or out, no one asked questions. Rumors spread of a town overrun with the walking dead. This once beautiful, blighted village was left on their own to fester in this curse.

At this story, Lario stood up enraged and demanded that they change course. "We can't go to my home, the mob will be waiting for us there. Anyways, how could I go home and hide knowing what you've told us." More than that, Lario needed to know if he was responsible. He needed to see the Lariosauro with his own eyes. "Please, we need to go to Raven's Cove and confront this terrible curse."

And so the three men changed course to the distant cove. And it wasn't long before the boat slowed, as Captain Charn had warned, into the black oily water of the dank lagoon. As foretold, black birds and crabs wrestled in piles, all pecking viciously at each other, making ungodly cries that echoed along the shadow of the mountain. The ferryman dropped his sails and began firing his engine back up, eager not to linger. "There's nowhere to moor and we cannot get trapped in this thick soup, we'll never get out."

Meanwhile, Lario stood frozen at the bow, confronted with the ruins of a once perfumed and flowered village, the aftermath of his own sin. This blighttown was cursed and shadowed by something beyond bad luck. Some evil fate was seething in spiteful misery and spewing her madness. Lario immediately felt the familiar weight of his own abandoned sorrows, its stench lingering heavy in the air. He knew it was his old forgotten coin left behind causing this cascading rot. This evil force of neglected worry, the festering of reckless abandonment. And as he glanced around at the bubbling foam across the water, Lario suspected something wicked was indeed below, busy growing her ruthless jaws in the depths.

Lario felt a pinch in his stomach, something he hadn't felt since that one fateful day. He was brimming full again with worry and regret. "What have I done? Surely I will carry this hefty guilt my entire life!" As his voice carried along the water, there was a returning echo that was not his own. Rather a low gurgling bellow that rumbled deeply in the stomachs of the entire crew.

Answering Lario's tormented cries, out of the hot frothy water, rose a familiar head, the head of the mighty Lariosauro. It was smooth like a seal, but she had grown more gnarly, green-scaled and terrible. Her attention was fixated solely on Lario, as she rose higher from the black stench, steam pouring off her back, and tail whipping eddies all around her behemoth body. Lario broke his trance in time to suggest to the others they make an about turn and fast retreat.

"We're already two steps ahead of you," Santino had trimmed the mainsail for a forgiving tailwind and was now helping the captain with the spinnaker. "Cut the engines, there's a westerly wind that will serve us better. Back to Silica, I suppose."

Lario thought on that but a better plan stewed inside him. "No wait, not there, back to mine, straight to that line of glowing torches." Lario pointed starboard to their heading, as they shifted from straight running to a broad reach.

"We might not get the same push if we're going to unrun her." Warned the captain.

"We're not going to unrun her, we're going to lure her out. It's time I confront this monster I've made and bring her to her knees. She's holding my bane, that old coin of mine, and I'm going to cut it out of her before the night is out." Lario rallied.

"Fight her? Are you mad? Did you not see the size of her," Santino shouted in a frenzy, as the vessel started to pick up speed. "It would take an army to take down that behemoth!"

"Right, or a mob. One full of bloodlust. Bring me to those marauders, we'll give them someone to fight. Someone worth fighting." Lario peered

over his shoulder as he helped trim the sails, seeing that frightful leviathan lashing her tail in fiery pursuit. "Dawn is upon us, and before the sun rises, we're going to kill this bane on our town. By God, we're going to kill this wicked beast!"

Part VIII: Slaying the beast of burden

As the tiny crew continued their retreat to Lario's home port, the vengeful beast pursued intently, lashing the waters into whirlpools that would impress Charybdis herself. Lariosaurio could have scuppered this fast scuttling ferry with any lash of her tail, but seemed to delight in toying with the crew. Lario stood at the bow and pointed the old captain towards the fast approaching shoreline. Unsurprisingly, the assembled masses of angry villagers were there waiting.

Santino had taken an oar out to push and weave around the scattered row boats moored in the cove, as they zigzagged their way inland. The anxious lynch mob rushed the waters, weapons in hand pillaged from a boarded up old boathouse, frenzied and eyes ablaze. The storehouse had been loaded with long harpoons and rusty whaling gear that looked to be a hundred years old, from an age when this glacial lake was connected to the sea and whale hunting was a popular trade.

The mob halted suddenly, knee deep in the beach tides, as their sights shifted from Lario to something impossibly more sinister rising out of the water behind him. Mouths agape and torches dropping into the water, the gang stood in disbelief as this ghastly lake monster perched up like a striking viper, unleashing a deafening sonic screech that sent ripples along the lake.

Lario rushed to shore amidst the armed band, shouting, "She's real, the Lariosauro is real! There's no time to explain. This is our curse and we must destroy her!" The posse quickly retrieved their harpoons out of the tide, putting themselves in motion, in favor of facing their own disbelief. "Gather any weapons we can find, nets and grappling hooks. And load them onto the old whaler boats."

Before he had even finished his orders, a veteran soldier and his sons were dragging an old chest of dynamite from their storage shed, and started firing rifles at the beast. As the titanic beast made a dashing retreat, further from shore, the sons distributed sticks of dynamite amongst the makeshift navy, who were now launching their assault boats in pursuit.

The sea turned into chaos, as a dozen small vessels took to the harbor, hurling explosions onto the rippling whitecaps, and circling the lashing fins of this mad kraken, Lariosauro. The heartiest fisherman of Silica and the surrounding villages all redirected their vengeance towards this new villain. But their hopeful comradery faded quickly as the beast dove deep and prepared to mount her counterattack. The scrambled assault halted, as the lakefolk held their breath, harpoons at the ready and eyes darted around the empty rocking waves.

Another high pitched sonic squeal pinched the nerves in their ears, and a long deep baritone followed, a horrible horn sizzling in their stomachs. Then, the water shattered into the air, raining down curtains across the crewed boats. The wraithful demon emerged from these watery drapes, reeling high and poised to strike. Diving and jumping, her trailing body wove through the scattered fleet like she meant to stitch them together. Her deadly tail whipped and bashed the sides of the small boats apart. Her scaly green head snapped fierce jaws at the sailors tossed overboard, wading and clutching feebly for their harpoons.

Among them was Lario, scrambling to a capsized skiff and pulling himself onto its wobbly dome, spear still desperately in hand. Santino treaded water next to him with Captain Charn, both panicked, as the beast began to circle. The dizzy waves made it difficult for Lario to balance, as this demon stirred destruction all across the lake. He tried to pull Santino and the ferryman up with him, but they were busy muttering cries for mercy.

"Oh lord, please don't let me die like this. I never got to mend my fence. I never got to give my daughter's hand in marriage. I want to live, there is so much I cannot leave behind!"

The sea monster stopped toying with the other ships and now carved a deft path towards them with deadly resolve. But Lario was lost in the moment, ignoring the attack, caught up listening to his friend, so normally calm and in the moment, expressing fears he likely hadn't said out loud in ages. At that moment, Lario shared his best friend's concerns and said faithfully, "Santino, look at me, you're going to be OK."

At this, something unexpected caught Lario from the corner of his eye. A halt in the rippling waters, as the lake monster stopped dead in her own wake. Her neck spasmed and she shook side to side, as if she had been caught in some invisible net. Slowly drifting through hot air bubbles, she raised her head up higher to catch her breath. And then most unexpectedly, she let out a strange gulp.

Santino calmed his frantic wading and looked to Lario in disbelief. "Did you hear that? Did she just… hiccup?"

Lario nodded and started puzzling it out, "What were you muttering about, Santino, say those things again. Say them now!"

"Um, I would but I'm a bit busy worrying about drowning at the moment, my friend." Santino fretted.

"Quickly please! You were listing out all those problems, the ones you keep to yourself!"

"Well, my daughter's still unwed, my sons I fear might get drafted. Let me see, is this what you mean?" Santino paddled a bit, and started rambling to himself.

And again, the Lariosauro started to gag and convulse a bit, as she waved her long neck higher over the water, towering above Lario's upturned skiff.

"Right, go on! All those things you chew on each night, the ones that *really* keep you tossing and turning. Keep talking."

Santino almost forgot he was treading water, busy counting on his fingers, "Well, I don't want to leave any debts behind, and hell, there's the book I always promised to write. I've spent so much time at the cafe, I haven't had the chance to... is this really the time for this, Lario? ... to make amends with my wife."

Lario fixed his eyes sharply on the lake beast now rocking side-to-side in agony. He immediately tagged in, listing out all his old worries, the ones he had buried for so long. The sorrows he had thought abandoned. And the beast's attention turned squarely on him.

"And me, I wish I was smarter. I worry I'm not fit to finish anything at all. I worry about my money growing thin, along with my hair. I worry that I'm losing my friends. And I worry most of all that I'll die alone and never be remembered."

That was the final punch. Lariosauro roared again, but this time, it seemed to come from deep inside her belly. A rumbling gurgle vibrated across the lake and across the surrounding foothills. And then, the monster opened her mouth wide and let out a gigantic, mountain clattering, cloud breaking belch! "BURRRRRRP!"

And while the villagers swam about desperately, they couldn't help but pause to exchange confounded looks. Lario knew he wasn't in the clear just yet. The monster shook her head a little and began licking her teeth in discomfort. Her eyes found Lario and she knew her tormentor immediately. Her slick humpback rising like an island in a draining bathtub, a whirlpool forming around her. Another loud screech, whether from gas or berserk rage, she was more resolute than ever to come eye to eye with Lario.

Lario knew what he had to do, and he would only have one shot at this. He gripped his spear tightly and called for the monster. His bane and his soul ready for a splintering collision. "Come for me, great demon of old, bearer of my sorrows. End my life with your wicked teeth, free yourself from your pain. Bite swiftly. Destroy me. I am your tormentor!"

The monster's head dove like a giant bird of prey, jaws open wide. Lario stood steady as he could on the rocking skiff. Then pulling his long harpoon back far with a strong arm, he prepared a fierce thrust. Eyes darting around for a target: an eye, the tongue, or even straight down the dragon's throat. And then Lario saw it, the shimmering reflection between the teeth of the lake creature. There in front of him, wedged tightly like a toothpick between sharp teeth, was his gold coin. He recognized it immediately and could feel its weight in the pit of his stomach. There was no time to get lost in marvel and without hesitation, Lario let loose his spear, finding the space between those snapping teeth and dislodging the coin.

Liberated, the little gold curse flew high and hot into the air, as both Lario and the old beast followed its arc with a connected gaze. But it was Lario that leapt first and snatched the coin out of the twilight sky. It sizzled and charred his hand, as he gripped it hard. Searing his hand like a cast iron panhandle, he could not take it any longer and released it. Lario cradled his arm and dropped to his knees, watching the coin plummet into the depths.

The coin fell fast and heavy. And the Lariosauro plunged desperately in pursuit, ignoring Lario and the men. She did not know why, but this curse, this tormentor, was not something she was ready to release. So this once gentle old dinosaur dove deep and swift after her coin.

When the coin hit the lake floor, an earthquake echoed back, rocking the mountain's base and the surrounding shores. The basin floor split open into a great chasm, and still the coin fell farther. The Lariosauro chased her golden lure with fervent obsession, squeezing through the seabed ravines. Dormant channels opened wide and wove cavernous rivers endlessly into the deep abyss below the Alps. And so it was, the

Lariosauro went lost through this maze of the unknown, madly chasing her fleeting bane.

Meanwhile, Lario swam to the surface, finding his brethren scattered but treading safely. He collected them one by one, locking arms, and eventually leading the entire lot back to shore. Two young were even seen helping old Captain Charn onto his feet and reveling in their victory. No one could see the shadow of the monster any longer through the murky water. And the golden glow of Lario's coin had faded from the land. But as Lario cradled his crippled hand, he noticed a circular scar with the coin's markings branded clearly on his palm. And that gave him comfort.

Part IX: Scars of the unclenched

Lario rubbed at the old blistered scar on his hand thoughtfully at the Onice Nero. It itched from time to time, even on warm summer nights like tonight. But the discomfort was made tolerable by grasping a cold pint of ale, sitting around the patio campfire, and listening to the tales of his huddled friends.

It had been almost a year now since that day when he sought to reclaim his coin, and instead freed a wrathful beast and the burdens of Silica. Each month, the village grew more vibrant in the returning sunshine. Idle hands found new purpose, and nervous chatter waned to cheerier tales. The lakefolk found forgiveness for each other, turning their backs on the dark days, as they united to rebuild their paradise village.

Lario's name ensured a fate of *'depth and reflection.'* However, he recalled that his last name, Bonaventure, meant *'good fortune.'* And perhaps he could find a purpose serving this town, ensuring that good fortune would indeed return.

It wouldn't be without toil, and there was always time for gripes and gossip. Luckily, Lario was there to listen to the troubles, always leading the conversation with optimism and empathy. And always making time each evening, quietly listening to the good people of Silica. Just like Santino had taught him to do.

Lario would sometimes spare a thought for the poor old Lariosauro. He wondered if she had dove fast enough to catch his old coin. Then he would glance down at the small circle on his palm and hope that she had found a better path. One that would give her freedom from her troubles and the burdens of men. As he had found himself.

Lario shook off the thoughts on his itchy scar and decided to close his palm warmly on the shoulder of his friends around the table. He grinned and leaned in closer to hear the tales of wonders and worries. These were the tiny moments, finding commonality, that made his soul sing again. And although it took a horrible little coin to teach him what to abandon and what to embrace, he knew now one's affect on others was the only true currency.

Epilogue: Just another seafaring beast

Deep off the coast of the Mediterranean sea, swam a lumbering old lake monster in unfamiliar waters. It had been a year of searching through that underground maze of cavernous rivers beneath the mountains. It had been one year since she had left her home near the town with those curiously peculiar upright apes. It had been one year since she lost the bane of her gold coin.

Lariosauro had spent her days, chasing after that silly old coin, in the river depths, through forgotten caverns, dazed and engulfed with a feverish longing. It took some time to relent to her loss, and let go of the rage she had held so stubbornly. And even though she had thought it was the pain that had made her stronger, it wasn't until it was lost forever that she found a different strength.

As her burdens withdrew, eventually her fever began to cool. As her body grew graceful again, she resolved to abandon her search. She found inside herself the blossoming of something else long lost, a sense of wonder and curiosity. And for the first time in her century old life, Lariosauro found the desire for a new adventure, a new home, and a reason for being.

After many months, puzzling her way out of that maze of flooded tunnels, she was at last in the open sea. Compared to the place she called home her whole life, she was in awe of the sea's endlessness. So many unseen horizons in every direction, so many choices ahead. There were fresh schools of delicious fish abound, with which she immediately filled her belly. She grew strong again and turned one last time to the tunnel that led back to the home she would never return.

Instead she would push west to explore these endless horizons. West to the Atlantic ocean, where she found the horizons as unlimited as her opportunities. She only needed to make a simple choice on what would be next. A choice to find new adventures and new connections. Maybe she'll make friends closer to her age. Well maybe not age, but size for sure. Perhaps she could find those blue whales her fishes were always yammering about.

Or perhaps even still, she could meet another old dinosaur like herself. A companion with whom to share her stories. Someone to listen to that she could finally understand. Wouldn't that be a treasure worthy of a good journey? She recalled old stories about the deep lakes up north in a place called Scotland. So the Lariosauro decided that might be a good place to start.

Sisyphus Goes Job Hunting

A reimagined Greek myth
with guest artwork by
Ted C. Wiedenman

Sisyphus Goes Job Hunting, *a reimagined Greek myth*

Part I: The Rock & Roll King

The tall, thin ghost of a king gasped in pause halfway up the cliffside, calloused hands planted firmly on his craggy old boulder, weighing the risks to wipe the salty sweat off his sun-squinted eyes. He looked at his raisin-wrinkled arms and down to his loose tattered tunic. He anchored his sinewy legs into a lunging braced position that wedged his right knee deep into this mighty rock ahead. He breathed quickly in and out, getting ready for his next maneuver. He had done this many times before with mixed results. The trick was to ensure his footing was dug under, not on top of, all of this loose shalestone. Then, he would lean forward hard to lay his left forearm flush and low against the boulderface. Next, one last jutting wedge of his knee for stability, then heave with all his godly might.

The stone-skinned immortal, named Sisyphus, let out a large cry from sharp pain in his spine. And the burning embers inside his thighs matched the heat from his sun-scorched skin. He slowly lifted his right hand into the air, while ignoring a drop of blood twisting its way down his knee. And with the grace of a swooping osprey, Sisyphus sponged his forearm across his sweaty brow for one sweet moment of fleeting relief. Heaven.

One tiny remission from his task. One small break from this stubborn rock and that impassable ridge. It wasn't much of a relief, and hardly worth the pain it caused in his knee. But he still sighed to mark the moment of something different. A small treasured moment, to store in the treasure chest he kept in his mind's castle. A new addition to his fortress of hope.

As he lingered, his revels betrayed him, and his feet skidded out along the loose pebbles. Left knee now pestling into gravel, he fumbled to get both hands anchored firm again, as the boulder ploughed him two meters down the mountainside. His feet cut into sharp stone, and his ankles twisted about, as he lost another three meters. Down and down he went, before finally swinging around in desperation, slamming his back flat into his terrible boulder and bringing her retreat to a halt.

"Dammit, me!" Sisyphus yelled, peering down the gravity well of the basin, where his rock longed to be. Hours of the day lost, but could've been worse. He looked over his shoulder up, up and up, towards the ridge. Although he had failed many times for countless years to reach that spiny crest, he saw up there his life's longing, his most desired ambition.

Was it the longing for relief? Maybe. The desire for finality? He wasn't sure. But his days were filled by the dreams of what awaited at that summit. The chance to let the boulder rest, the chance to push it down the other side. Damned be Zeus, maybe there would just be another higher mountain on the other side. But still, it would be something new, a break from this routine.

The god king Sisyphus shuffled his feet upwards through razer-blade shale flakes. His setback had attracted the ravens, always there to feed off his failure, circling and cawing their taunts into his unprotected ears.

"Kraa-kraa, failed again, Sisyphus!" Their throaty cries mocked. *"Kraa-kraa,* it's only a matter of time before you drop this one. *Kraa.* Why do you even try? *Kra-Kraa-kra,* there is nothing at the top! Surrender and sleep, Sisyphus, *sleeeeep!!"*

He'd sometimes wave them off, or spit at them as they pecked away at his neck and ribs. But today, he just endured and pushed his boulder a little further. Afterall, he's had worse tormentors in his many lives. Worse naysayers to shrug off. And things in general, had been and could be worse.

Sisyphus busied himself back up the familiar path, changing small grips, making small footing attunements, shifting his weight around. To pass the time, he started to recall the moments that got him here and the lesson he was meant to learn.

"For cheating death, I sentence you to an eternity of rolling this boulder up a mountain, ever failing, for all of time", Zeus had proclaimed. It all seemed a large overaction, Sisyphus thought. Had he *really* cheated? Or was the god of gods just being sensitive because he had outsmarted them all?

When he made that deal with some river god, all seemed fair and agreed upon. Sisyphus gave up something precious that Zeus had hidden away and only he knew about. He knew Zeus' secret, but never really swore an oath to keep it. So he gave it over in exchange for endless prosperity in his life. Heavy rains for his lands, bountiful harvests, countless riches for his kingdom, that sort of thing. River gods had a way with water, afterall. Seemed to be a fair enough trade.

Well, Zeus didn't take it well, but how was that cheating death? If anything he was guilty of greed, but as king, he planned to share it all. If that was a crime, where were the millions of other kings of humanity along this mountain? Where were their boulders? Had Zeus confused the two things, desire for prosperity and desire for immortality? Wouldn't be the first person, I suppose.

Sisyphus shook off his dwelling in the past, his replays never really got him anywhere. He decided to play a different game to pass the time, recalling the many lives his spirit had experienced, drifting through different people in this task, and sharing his torment with other mortals through the ages. He went back to a previous thought, just a moment ago, "Things had been and could be worse". Indeed, it was true. Like the time he had lived the life of that odd little twenty-first century tech executive, stuck in perpetual unemployment in a down economy.

Part II: A Fate Far More Tedious

The tales of Sisyphus and his torment were spread far and wide through the ages of man. All would know of the cost for cheating death. Or for betraying a god? Or, for making a clever prison break, maybe? Actually not many people really understood what the moral of his story was. And many were left scratching their heads to understand if the punishment truly fit the crime. Every day this disgraced king of old was humiliated to push the same boulder up a mountain painfully, begrudgingly, thanklessly, ending each day in failure and frustration.

And each and every time, he would find only the small flicker of hope as he neared the crest of this impassable mountain. Only to feel the boulder slip from his hands, inevitably, as he lamented its rolling descent back to the beginning. Countless times, over and over... forever. Why would he climb back down? Why would he start over? Why expect a different result at each try? Why would he not give up forever? Only Sisyphus knew.

Woe was the bane of King Sisyphus. And each ascending attempt was a little different, each a little trickier than the last. Sometimes he would make it halfway, sometimes he'd slip just at the ridge. Sometimes he would spend all day just getting the boulder started. He had even tried running up the path alone to see what was over that blasted ridge, but would slip and get yanked back by some invisible tether. So he would sigh, dust himself off, and try again.

Only he knew why, it was said. Well, that was only a half truth. For it was his duty to not just suffer this one failed assignment, but to share this pain with millions of others throughout time, those who have ever felt as he did at a thankless task.

And that is why Sisyphus often amused himself, phasing into other people's lives, like throwing on a movie, to see what other souls he was tangled up in. And they were quite amusing tales indeed. Like the man serving an innocent man's sentence in solitary confinement for over twenty years. Although compared to a boulder, that was a piece of cake. There was also the one poor soul trapped in a collapsed foxhole during WWII, spending months trying to dig his way through dead enemy soldiers and fallen comrades. At last that man had purpose and an end goal in sight. And who could forget the misery he had witnessed across five years, spent married to a Hollywood actress. That was truly miserable. Can you imagine?

Many lives Sisyphus had spent hopping from his one boulder to someone else's. And through them all, perhaps the worst one still was the two years he spent as that absurdly stubborn, ungratefully successful businessman. Maybe it wasn't the worst in terms of torture and suffering, but it was the one that confounded his senses the most, and shook his very notions of happiness. And he had been a king of vast riches in his own day. So it was really saying something that he was confounded the most by this one man named Will, the king of his era, whom he found himself returning to often.

Sisyphus learned a lot about the twenty-first century and the western world through the lens of Will. He was the epitome of modern lavishness, the people of this time. Everyone had an incredible sense of individualism and self-obsession. And convenience and entertainment were the riches of the day. And by that, everyone seemed convinced they were kings and queens, no matter their station.

But top of the food chain were the hustlers. The real royalty at this time, those who could imagine something and then just make it happen. The people that prized career and achievement above all else. And there was no better hustler than the 'born from nothing' career king named Will.

Will had more ambition than blood flowing through him. He was really good at influencing and leading large teams at the companies of the world. Which Sisyphus didn't find too unfamiliar from his days of trying to lead by example as a generous king. And like the old Greek King, Will prided himself on being firm but fair. Equally respected and revered. His loyalty to others seemed to come with a shelf-life that spoiled in the wake of his goals. Or stated another way, he was endearing when he wanted to be. And a bit of a prick the rest of the time.

Will was a solo artist, able to pick up and move cities or countries at the drop of a hat in his pursuit to keep climbing the career ladder. He worked in the booming prosperity of the technology business, climbing the ranks to be a senior exec for one of the most valuable tech conglomerates in the world. In this era, the kings were not measured by their possessions or heritage so much as their accomplishments and abilities, it would seem. And Will's resume of achievements was strong.

Will had carved out his track record for building teams, and leading them through trust and expertise, not sovereignty or power. He did not conquer armies or cities, but he expanded his empire by navigating complex challenges, gaining profit for his company, and thereby status. His kingdom was fully measured by his reputation and ability to achieve. Even though these called companies were not violent, make no mistake there were still conquests to be had. And wealth and luxury often followed from the spoils of these victories. Some things never change with kings.

So imagine Will's sense of shock and betrayal, at the peak of his kingdom, the peak of his conquests, almost infallible in his conquests, that he suddenly found himself without job or title. He wouldn't be the first king to fall from grace, or be mutinied against. But Will still found a unique betrayal in knowing the world's economic tides had taken an unforeseen turn that knocked him into a state he had never known. Helpless and unemployable. Sisyphus knew immediately why he had been summoned into this man's life. And recognized immediately the long, thankless road that laid ahead, even if Will did not yet.

Part III: Pushing a Resume up a Mountain

Something that always fascinated Sisyphus, living through Will's eyes, was how little you needed to survive in this age, yet how desperately everyone scrambled for more. In his kingdom of old, everyone seemed a bit calmer knowing their station, from senator to peasant. The true sin of this New Age seemed to be the false illusion casted down to every human being that they all mattered in every single way.

But not Will, his sin wasn't that he believed he was better than he was. He was just wired to overreach, and could never stop wanting more. Climbing to a high peak of kingliness, traveling lavishly, commanding with authority, waking when he wants, eating and drinking what he wants, unbound and unrestricted in his lifestyle. The liberty and insulation of a wealthy bachelor in his prime. Only to watch it all dissolve in front of him, as the tides of an economy turned during a global pandemic that heightened the people's sense of caution. And corporations could not afford to take any unnecessary risks.

Will was a rounding error on a spreadsheet now, and found himself in unchartered waters. He was asking for special consideration and being ignored by the world passing by. He was asking for new opportunities, and for the first time in his life, was being told *"No"!* He fired off dozens of applications into the ether, and waited for the offers to come pouring in, in high praise for his golden resume. He waited and listened for the applause. And what returned was silence.

Sisyphus felt the toils, seeing each one of Will's fired off job applications as its own heavy boulder. And Will was starting to feel as the mighty immortal once felt, a disbelieving betrayal, as each of the first boulders slipped uncontrollably, failingly, down to the beginning.

Will sat himself diligently each morning shackled to his home office desk. With one single purpose every day, he gripped his desperate fingers to his laptop and pushed his resume up a daunting slope. Each application, its own process. Each turn of the boulder, a new set of research and preparation. Each company, a new tailored business plan and presentation. Each effort, uniquely and precariously gaining momentum, climbing higher, and with further to fall.

Whenever Will neared the final rounds of each interview process, he would feel some new swell of hope. Jumping through hoops, relaying charming leadership anecdotes, highlighting the accomplishments of his past. Then he could feel his hands shaking with excitement, as he rounded the bend for a job offer. He would get a taste of it, if only by imagination, of what future spanned beyond the horizon, and what he would become in this new role, this new company, this new life!

Then, unexpectedly, something would fall from his grip. And the dreaded automated email would come through with the familiar keywords like *"despite your background"* and *"there were many other experienced candidates"* and *"unfortunately, at this time"*. So Will's hard effort would be lost, rolling back down the mountain, where he would trudge along and start again.

Sisyphus could feel the familiar perils and hear the seeds of doubt looming. Like those ravens and buzzards pecking and squawking at him with such fierce cruelty.

"Kra-Kra... How did this happen to you of all people? Kra! How did you not see this coming? Kraa-Kra! Maybe you've just been lucky your

whole life. Kraaa! Maybe you're going to need to lower your standards! Kraaa! Kraaaaa!

Will would wave these buzzing setbacks away. He remained determined to suffer the loss, draw his own conclusions, dust himself off, take a deep breath, and start again. What Sisyphus found most fascinating was how many of these boulders Will could juggle at once, when he had only the one. All different sizes, all anchored at different spots up the mountain side. Will divided his energy shifting from one application to another, some would get stuck, while he waited for a callback, or a next step. Some would be small but get heavier as he rolled him uphill. Some became so immovable, he just wondered when they were going to roll back on their own. And so impatiently he would kick them down himself.

Sisyphus watched Will getting strong, more clever with his grip, as he had done. And although he pitied him, he was also learning a little about his own strife by watching Will's stubbornness. The ancient lord of punishment began to see how sometimes achievement was not really in one's control. Perhaps that's the advice he wished he could pass along. *"Put your hubris aside, modern King Will, this is not up to you. The gods will decide when it's time to hit that ridge. If it is in your stars at all."*

Part IV: Interlude for Revelation

Back on the mountain, Sisyphus made one mighty turn of his tectonic rock that would've impressed Atlas himself. He took a breather and pondered his advice for both Will and himself. What were the crimes that got him here again? He just couldn't help replaying this strange predicament, hoping it was some elaborate riddle waiting to be solved. He knew if he buttoned his attention up, he could figure this out once and for all. So he cleared his mind of Will for a minute, and he ran down the facts as he knew them.

First he made a deal with some river god to gain eternal harvests and prosperity for his city. Fine, that was greedy. But again, he did it for the prosperity of all his citizens. One might call that magnanimous! Then he recalled having to, *sort of*, betray the god of gods, Zeus in the process. What was the hidden prize again? Something about the location of his favorite collection of beautiful river nymphs. Is that really betrayal? 'Boo-hoo!' Sorry you lost your pervy little harem of secret nymphs!

Also, wasn't one of them the daughter of the same river god? So one would say I was a hero for helping a father find his daughter. Sisyphus would've made the news as a hero in the modern day. OK, then, in Zeus' temper tantrum, he had Sisyphus killed and sent to Hades. A bit harsh, but one might guess kings have been killed for less.

Sisyphus was pleased at this little recall game, and it seemed he was making good progress on his boulder turns in its distraction. So he was down in Hades, he remembered. Dead, of course. Oh right, and the next part he would admit not being too proud of. But well, let's just say the warden of Hades, Death, had it coming. Death was a pretty prince and had a lot going for him, but sharp witted, he was not. So Sisyphus maybe, kind of, tricked him into testing and wearing the prison chains that were meant for him. He supposed, in a way, that it was sort of *'cheating death'*. But is it really cheating, when it's that easy to outwit a moron? Would you call the best poker player at the table a cheater? No, just clever.

Sisyphus shook his head, while rolling his rock another sweet degree, his anger and disbelief spurring him forward. So there it was again, was he really being punished for being too clever? Zeus was clearly not going to take a prison break from Hell gracefully. But the next time he got caught, well, it all just felt a bit personal.

The unexpected consequence of his first escape, leaving Death trapped in chains, wasn't just *him* cheating death. Apparently, *all the people* in the world were robbed of their chance to die. He had robbed humanity in that moment of the glory of short life and the chance to embrace their fear of death. And of all the gods to not to cross, it was the *'god of war'* that took this most poorly. War, apparently, is not an entertaining sport if no one can die. So it was Ares in the end that hunted Sisyphus down and swiftly cast him back down, where he himself freed Death, and put the chains back where he deserved.

Dropped back into Hades, this time Sisyphus knew he wasn't going to stay, no matter the risk. He had to use his wiley charms on the kind-hearted wife of Hades, Persephone. He convinced her that his wife back home was misled into thinking he was not dead from the confusion of before. Therefore, she would offer no prayers or funeral offerings. Therefore, no presents for Hades for all this effort.

Well, yeah, so he lied... to a goddess. And maybe it was that straw that broke Zeus' back. Fathers can get a bit protective of their daughters. So when he found Sisyphus, once again, lounging and mocking the gods from his old high castle, the final sentence came swift and terrible. And that's how Sisyphus came to be shackled to this boulder, never able to escape, always with this burning desire to press forward. No notion of defeat, no sense of accomplishment. Nothing but the infinite frustration of seeking. Aspiration without results. Trials without consequence.

And although it had been uncounted centuries passed, he can still recite the words Zeus said at his trial. He remembered Zeus seeming weary and resigned as he proclaimed,

"Sisyphus, you count the gods among your peers, you cheat your very destiny as if you are more clever than them. You long only to return to your human city, and to continue to build yourself this endless wealth. You loathe the finality of death, yet you tick off your achievements and conquests so flippantly in life. Sisyphus, I wish to help you understand what you are seeking without knowing it. I feel it is my duty to give you the endless life you so long for."

Part V: Crossing the Impassable Crest

Back in the modern world, Will paused at his keyboard, as if a profound truth was just shot into his head. This year proved a true reality breaker when it came to his sense of invincibility. Each day feeling more certain that it was the world that had judged him a little too harshly. And what was his crime afterall?

It had only been a year now since he was in his prime. Of wealth, of influence, of relevance. And he gripped so desperately for a way to make his way back to that peak. He craved those little winks from the world, the sparks that kept him going. Whether a wink from a pretty girl from across the room, the admiration he got from his peers, or the honest appreciation he got from his team on a hard job done well. The hope of reclaiming that lifestyle kept him going during this grim year.

Will was imagining the old myth of Sisyphus in times like these. He loved picturing himself on that mountainside, trying to push his own boulders alongside him. And he was in awe at that woeful old ghost king's resolve. He wondered how that immortal tortured soul would handle each of these failed applications, rolling so disposable down the mountain. And how he was able to keep picking himself back up for the next round, when each of these rejections stung worse than the one before. Should this not be getting easier? Was he learning nothing?

So in this meditation, between myth and riddle, Will resolved to keep pushing, to find new ways to rebound after each failure. When all felt lost, he would pause and channel his brother in arms, his avatar of endless torment. Or was it endless hope? And just like that, it occurred to Will why Sisyphus endured such misery over and over again. He imagined Sisyphus smiling as he did it.

Just as Will was waiting in agony for a response to his last interview, he suspected Sisyphus was also wincing in sad anticipation for his next dropped boulder. Just as Will had delayed the embarrassment of opening another *thanks but no thanks'* email, he expected Sisyphus also to be burying his head in the sand. Except, he wasn't. Will has a much clearer picture of a happy Sisyphus now than ever before. Enjoying the turns, expecting the best, moving forward in perpetual, immortal hope.

Will could see Sisyphus now, as if he was peering through a window to that hellish mountain slope. He could see him lose his grip and watch with acceptance as his boulder bustled past him, once again, charging back to lowland's ravine. He could see the titan king showing content and even a small chuckle at the inevitable, sighing a little as he shuffled his callus bare feet down after it. Back to the beginning. And Will wondered if he could ever feel that happy with his next failure. What if, just what if, he could replace that low pitted angst, with a wash of relief and readiness for the next trial? What if he could fail without the sting?

Afterall, why should it feel like such a gut punch every time? Had he even cleared one single boulder over that ridge? One single job application after hundreds? Which was the greater sign of madness, expecting something to change while giving the same effort or yearning to understand how to fail better?

It became more and more clear that his year had not been about finding a job. It had been about the grace and dignity to perpetually dust himself off and starting anew. With each tiny new job prospect he found, each accepted application into a new stage, he felt born again. A new opportunity, someone taking interest, a new interesting interview, a like-minded peer, some glimmer of hope. And that hope was rebuilding him.

Will settled into this thought, and understood what his friend had already found, a cure for hubris. It was hubris, after all that was their shared crime. Not greed, nor dishonesty, nor blasphemy. It was their corrupted pride, twisted into thinking their luck was owed, that it was theirs and theirs alone. Will knew it was the great myth of this century, as people rode the waxing and waning tides of wealth, fooling themselves into thinking they decide their own fates.

Will decided at that moment to break free by releasing his clutched control. He stopped bracing for the next disappointment, and he found a new peace in seeing each of his boulders in various stages along the path. He picked one that he had been ignoring for too long, and decided to give a few more turns, to return a voicemail that he knew was more bad news. And on the call, the recruiter did in fact fall into their typically familiar rejection script, generically running through their feedback. Ravens swooping in, squawking and excited for their feeding frenzy. But this time, like kicking the boulder down the hill himself, Will cut it off.

"Actually, let me stop you there, I gather I'm not progressing and I'm relieved. Let's just agree we weren't a good fit for each other. Given both our expertise, I would hope our paths will cross again. No hard feelings, ok?"

Will ended the call, watched the boulder bustle by, and found his stubborn ego melting away. If his resistance was what was causing the pain, he would learn to let it all go. The ravens would keep seeding doubt in his ears, but he would laugh and listen to their silly songs. Anything to break up the time between pushing boulders.

Will started to give more variety to his days than the usual hustle and grind of job hunting. He found satisfaction in writing out business plan ideas. He took courses in fields that he might never pursue. And he took more meetings with old coworkers who could offer him nothing in return, just to hear their own experiences in these tough times. He felt stronger in finding some range and new interests. And yes, he kept rolling a few resumes up the mountain for the roles that really interested him.

Will enjoyed a few more days of present minded peace, until his phone rang again. He still had a lot of applications floating out in the world, old ones and new ones, content to let them play out their course without him. So it seemed unusual that this phone call drew his attention back to his imagined mountainside, to the vision of one very large, almost forgotten rock. Along the ridgeside, stood one job opportunity he had given up on months ago, but was now rolling a little on its own. Whether by a gust of wind, or a pestering raven, by the grace of persistence, or in spite of it... that boulder seemed loose and ready to push again. Will raced to grab it and embraced it with hopeful open arms. And then a whisper came, a friendly voice from his phone, a call from a company he almost forgot.

"Will, do you remember us? We just finished our budget cycle, and we haven't forgotten you. Is now a good time?"

***

Something over his shoulder caught his eye, and he saw the titan king's silhouette, pushing boulders alongside him. Will's surroundings had blurred, his desk, his phone, his computer screen, vanished. There was only the mountain slope now. Crows buzzing around from a far, foothold strong against loose terrain, a heavy boulder in his grip, and the ridge's crest now just an arm's length away. And Sisyphus was right beside him, in the flesh, and cheering him on. "Come on, kid! One last push, we got this!"

United in their task, the two souls arched their backs, kicked out their knees, and with a rally cry, both cleared the crest, onto a smooth, tabletop summit. And there the two men stood at the rooftop of the world, open horizons in all directions, panting exhaustedly, and grinning ear-to-ear. Will turned to face the stoic stone giant of Sisyphus, who was resting his head and forearm on a vastly larger boulder. Sharing their accomplishment, they both took a moment to marvel at the cloudtops from this vantage, heavens stretching endlessly below them. As Sisphus caught his breath, he nodded approvingly at Will, glancing from the clouds, then back down to the valleys below. There at their feet were countless new mountains, new low valleys, and all their punishing new slopes, stretching to infinite. And Will would've felt a quiver of dread, it weren't for Sisphus' revelling smile.

The summit vistas were breathtakingly precious but fleeting. The open sun began to cook them, and the wind started to pick up, signaling to Will they could not linger long. And so Sisyphus took the lead, by throwing his strong leg up onto his boulder and began to rock it back and forth. And with a sly wink, he nodded for Will to follow. Will pushed hard towards this new northern mountain slope, ready to begin again, as he was instructed. And just as his boulder rotated with enough force to turn down the mountain, Sisphus abruptly pulled back on his boulder, taking it back down the more familiar southern ridge. And the two souls parted ways down their different slopes, gleefully and giddily, chasing after their boulders to their respective basins.

Epilogue: Imagine a Smiling Immortal

Indeed Sisyphus went chasing down his lonely mountain pass, parting ways once and for all with Will. Unlike Will, he would remain on this mountain, but with a perspective unlike any mortal man could wish for.

He shared a lesson on hubris with Will, and the countless other soul's in limbo, when they were truly listening. Prosperity for its own sake is not a sin. He could say confidently now that his crime initially was not being greedy, or deceptive, or disloyal. It was in thinking himself too good for the natural order of the world. A longing for sustained prosperity, in the way only a god can ever know. Gods, incidentally, who are envious of the fleeting joys and the romantic fires of short burning mortality.

Alas, there was a difference between the two of these entangled souls, and the two wisdoms that were granted that day. For Will, it was truly the fear of failure that caused him to fumble, especially at the cusp of a meaningful achievement. He did find his breakthrough moment at last, once he was more free to forget himself, letting self-consciousness fade to vapor.

Sisyphus knew, better than most, that in Will's small rejections, there was something pure. A grace in tiny failures that gave the world beauty. If his penance was his humility, then his grace was in finding simple beauty in every new beginning.

Just as he helped Will along his journey of acceptance to move on with his life, Sisyphus learned from Will too. Zeus' punishment had turned out to be a gift. The gift of purpose without end. Purpose without reward. Purpose for its own sake.

So now imagine a smiling Sisyphus, as he shakes the dream of Will out of this head. Living out that modern man's life, caught in a thankless loop, confusedly, madly grasping for power and relevance, only to have those sand grains slip indifferently through his fingers. Woe be the fools of that era, that dream, thinking that the next mountain slope will be different, the next summit everlasting.

Imagine the wash of relief on this tired king's face, returning to the slow steady rolling boulder in front of him, a hopeful crest above. As he looks behind, then forward, ravens squawking playfully about, he feels the trials of the millions upon millions of mortal lives, working so hard to learn the lesson he had. And now imagine Sisyphus as he glances back down at his own two feet and his mammoth boulder, content to whisper verily, *"Oh, thank god, I'm not them."*

A tribute to The Myth of Sisyphus, a 1942 essay by french philosopher Albert Camus.

The Haunting of Mr. Query, *a gothic tale*

It was an autumn of lamentations, the day I broke my fell stare from pale rain-stained windows. My name is Franklin Arthur Query of the House of Query, the last of my line. I was spending my waning days scratching at the bones of the past, a withered lonesome crow in the hallowed derelict halls of my family's once great manor. A blight swept the neighboring farmlands and consumption had claimed many lives, including that of my dear wife Abigail. The oily fog of death still lingered but for some reason had yet to take me. The only plague I now feared was the festering question of 'when?'

Hovered over scantily laid parchment, resolved to finish my memoirs, I reached at last to dip my pen. And then, a pinch. A sharp pinch at my hand. From what, I had no inkling. Until a small scurry dove over the ledge of my bureau. A spider? Oh I prayed not, for I loathed the creepy trespasses of a spider lurking in dark spaces. I drew my dim candelabra under the table to investigate. Where did it go, that pesky pest? How did it get in here, that spinsterish scourge?

Too often now, these little puzzles came crawling from the invisible to disturb me. They were the constant reminder of uncertainty abound. It was these tiny invisible monsters who gripped me with skittish possession. Following every string of yarn at my fingers, fishing for truth, nothing would return to me but echoes of my empty castings. The curse of the unanswered niggled and taunted me, and at that moment, with the suspicion of some shapeless arachnid. Or worse, was it a rat?

A crack of thunder startled me, as hot wax sizzled droplets onto my bitten hand. I stood abruptly, sharply bumping my head on the table's edge. What was that? The howling gales churning into a thunder squall? Or some troubled thing stirring outside my forest's edge? I raced feverishly to the drawing room, dressing gown flying their tattered kitetails. My hand wiped obscured film from the iron-framed windows, as another howl from afar cinched my stomach. What wickedness taunts me? A fox, perhaps? Fiery and flearidden out pillaging my henhouse. Or a wolf? One with rabies, demented and ravaging my goats. Would I be deprived the taste of mutton, of butter, of eggs, this cold bleak winter?

A fresh thunderclap now rocked me back onto tilted heels, hands clutching crimson curtains, the driving reigns of crazed horses. Elm branches lashed against the dreary double panes and I petitioned them to cease their confounded wrapping. Could they shatter my false veneer of safety? Would their heavy limbs plunder fists upon my roof, leaving me penniless, freezing in hoveled corners?

I could no longer ponder so wearily at the sinister intentions of this squall. I fled to the kitchen, before the winds shaped themselves into some mad whirling deity. Despite my retreat from the leering windows, some frightful fiend seemed to follow me from the outside wall. The galley reeked heavy with the unattended kettle of mulled wine turned to vinegar. A bronze pot of four day old stew bubbled rancid. Had I eaten? How long had it been? The hanging herbs swarmed with black aphids and I longed to shoo them out a back garden door, which I dared not open. Had I remembered to lock it? Dare I test the latch?

Instead, I peeked through the transom window above the door. The overflowing river was pooling dark marsh into the garden beds, fording along the headstones of my sweet departed sons. What ghastly unrest would this roaring deluge unearth? Was I to bear witness to the walking dead, my ancestors dragging rotting legs from disturbed crypts to my doorstep? Would scratching nails drag me to hell at last? Why did I not kiss my wife and sons goodbye, to hold their hands in those feverish last moments? What terror had robbed me of my affections? How could I ever atone for such paralyzed absence? My eyes shut tight, defiant to the unfolding dark forest behind my back, pressed so coldly against the pantry door.

Frantically rubbing haunting illusions from my eyes, I was suddenly affronted by fresh devilries calling from the cellar stairs. Metal drums banged and clammored from the deep of my dank stone undercroft. Spitting steampipe screeches of fighting harpies below, as I walked towards the stairs delving into stone and fog. Had my furnace gone mad, churning and chewing on itself, mangling pipes and spitting fire upon the bones of my house? Had some cruel wraith made its den in the damp abyss, biding its time for wandering prey? These confounding questions, questions, questions - once again laying writhing parasites in my once peaceful head.

I could take no more of these itching inquiries and their petulant demands. I slammed the cellar door and sprinted to the grand foyer, neck hair raising higher with the breath of what was surely following. My steps quickened up winding stairs, while imagined yellow teeth nipped at my heels. Flesh-decayed hands reached between railing spindles for my ankles, as I made haste to the top floor and into the safe chambers of my master suite. Sharp lightning cast ghastly shadows of dancing goblins across soot-stained walls. My soul shrieked and my eyes dropped, as I dove under soft bed covers, burying my head from this veiled demon deceiver, surely closing in for the kill.

Under a duvet of hot breath, all was dark and all went quiet. The thunder stopped and I could hear no rain. Suddenly, I became acutely haunted by the new mysteries of compounding possibilities. Under quilted blinders, this crossroads of uncertainty was worse than any horror my eyes could conjure, and I was filled with every dreadful 'what, where and when' that could ever be. Would the unbearable unknowns consume me here, if I did not confront them? Could one die from terror alone? With mustered bravado, I cast off my sheets and touched feet to rickety floorboards. There in the stillness of an empty room, I spotted the spilling hypnotic light of a closet door left ajar. I crept softly towards it, my hand reaching for the doorknob, emboldened to give form to the formless.

My body was washed in crimson light, as I stared into the abyss of my closet. Towering above me, sprawling the expanding corners of my wardrobe, was the foulest of Lovecraftian demons staring back, enchanting me while time stood frozen. Enveloped by the choking vapors of sulfur and rum, this spawn of hell met my eyeline with burning basilisk damnation. A thousand eyes scattered around its wolf-spider head and squid-like tentacles wrapped into a hooded mane. Transfixed on its widening jaws, I leaned into rings of lamprey teeth, winding endlessly down its wormhole throat. At the pit of its stomach, I glimpsed the vacuous center of a lashing blackhole, greedily gobbling up suns and planets into a gravity well. Charmed by visions of oblivion, this ancient leviathan grappled my arms with stabbing fingers, pulling me into its slow consuming python mouth.

Before my final descent into this ninth gate of hell, where I was certain to spend perpetuity in vicious torment, swallowed by the infinite horror of finality, one last thought washed over me. Taking a final gasp of the stale manor's air, I whispered, 'Oh thank heavens, at last,' exhaling with surprising relief, 'an end to this query.'

A Banshee's Bargain, *an Irish ghost story*

PART ONE I was sitting at the pub with a pint of stout, a traveler's backpack nestled neatly under the barstool, reading a Yeats collection of poems about faeries. I was acting the part of a tourist, in between consulting gigs and taking the time to backpack around Europe. Despite my American appearance, I knew Dublin city like a native, and felt quite at home, as I settled through the afternoon into this cozy snug.

I've lingered here too long, as my quiet afternoon wanes into the raucous Saturday night crowds. My earbuds can't drown out the wailing of the messy hen party in the corner, as the spray-tanned British girls danced in a circle, shrieking and smashing gin & tonic goblets. From their hard-bitten country accents, they were likely from outside Yorkshire. No, maybe Newcastle. Yes, definitely that. I've been mixing with the Irish too long indeed if I could mistake the colorful Geordie-speak of northern England. They were clearly here on the 'lash,' so it was called, with their club-ready caked on makeup and wearing all manner of phallic bachelorette accessories.

I began to pack up and settle my tab, when my eyes got a little stuck. Captivated at first by the ridiculous drunkenness of the girls, but mystified more by the one bohemian girl that stood out, dancing around them. As they belted out the lyrics from the Spice Girls,, arm and arm spinning each other like a carousel, this one girl danced outside their circle, crowned with flowers around her cropped, strawberry blonde hair. She wore a tattered white slip against her ballerina-shaped silhouette. A large golden medallion hung low, framing her porcelain neckline and stoic features. There was something sad and almost terrifying about her detached playfulness, as she twirled about on, what I swear looked like, bare mud-crusted feet. And despite all this, she was quite plainly the most beautiful woman I had ever seen.

Regardless of her vagabond appearance, she carried a gentle grace as dancing and twirling outside the group. She would pirouette and bow in a way that seemed to taunt and mock the other girl's sloppy clamoring. She stayed strangely apart, tapping each one of them by the shoulder, a game of duck-duck-goose, then spinning herself around like a top after each pass with one finger to the top of her own head. I found myself leering fascinated, as I noticed she always seemed to skip the same person in her shoulder tap. I was completely hypnotized as I leaned out of my stool, swept up in the disbelief of her graceful dance.

It was at that moment when she abruptly planted her feet, gazed briefly at the floor before shooting her two green arrow eyes directly across the room to find me. She caught me staring and fired back in a way that give me a terrible shudder. I broke my stare but our eyes continued to peek and retreat, then dart around the room before sheepishly finding each other again. Each time, a little more inviting. The paused exchange was interrupted by the hoots and hollers from the girls. They were all finishing their round and pulling at each other's arms to head out to their next stop along the evening's city pub crawl.

The soft beauty whispered in each of their ears, as they scrambled abruptly to leave. So hurriedly in fact, they sent purses swinging about, spilling contents, and sailing at least three glasses to shatter on the floor. My trailing beauty walked over the glass in naked feet, unphased and unconcerned. She bent over to help collect one girl's scattered belongings, and seemed to catch her necklace on the corner of the table when she stood up. In her haste to leave with the group, she broke the chain on that necklace and sent it's hanging gold medallion spinning on the floor behind her, before scurrying past me.

The retreating Brits were being shouted at by the barkeep and the bar patrons as they made their exit. Seeing an opportunity, I leaped to scoop up the lost medallion and chased after my white-dressed enchantress to return it. Just as I was about to grab her arm, she spun around quickly and confronted me with a halted palm.

"How can you see me? It's not possible." I didn't understand her question, so I held up her lost pendent but she retracted, *"I cannot touch that, it was never mine in the first place. Please, you would be doing me a kindness to keep it."* Suddenly I was quite aware of a 'nothingness' around me. The music had seemed to stop, the room seemed a bit grayer, and the patrons were all frozen silent. I tried again to speak before she cut me off.

"Please, I am warning you, stand back." She rubbed the temples of her forehead in distress. *"It's my fault, I should not have let you see me. I should've never stared back. It's just, you just look so much like him. It's not possible."* Trailing off, she shook her thoughts away. I was so completely lost and confused, but feigned coolness, feeling content to stay in this moment forever, ensnared by her compassionate yet sullen voice.

Seeing my confusion, she tried again, *"To know me is to carry a curse, my fair lad. The coin is now yours, I cannot take it back, the dinner bell cannot be unrung. I fear tragedy will now be stalking your loved ones, and death will follow."* I wanted so much to laugh, wondering how much she had had to drink, but I just nodded away like a hopeless fool on a first date.

She looked back at me now with endearment, *"Perhaps we can make a deal. It is forbidden, but it is in my power to help you. You keep that gold coin from me, and in exchange I will try my best to keep Death off the scent of your family."*

I assumed she meant the medallion, as I felt its heaviness, and glanced down to see it's runic markings, noticing a pronounced pirate skull for the first time. Then my eyes snapped back up to clarify what she had said. Throat rattling a little, I asked her what she means by the death of my family?

"Listen closely now. Your aunt on your father's side will die in two days time. Don't ask me any more. Write down two names of your enemies, write it in black ink and place it folded in half under a glass you have sipped from. From there, my sweet love, I will do my best to bargain for her life on your behalf."

I was horrified by the hollow cold words in her morbid offer, and from such a sweet innocent face. Amidst my gasp, she turned back to the door and her company. I shook off my disbelief and attempted to grab her arm, pleading for her to explain. My arm stretched out for her, as she pressed out the door. I could see out the window the hen party, turning west along the river to town, sidewalks illuminated by lights along Samuel Beckett bridge. As I dove outside and turned in pursuit, something happened that I still cannot trust or expect anyone else to believe.

The streets had changed. The cars were gone, the bridge was gone. The paved motorway was replaced with cobblestone. There was a cold fog in the air. Horse drawn carriages were clacking about. Pedestrians were walking gingerly, couples draped in Edwarian fashion. Men with felt top hats and canes, women with plumed caps and draped in fur. I recognized the bustling livestock markets along the quays from something I had seen in faded photographs. And large steam fishing boats and transport ferries docked along the fresh stone banks. I looked around frantically for my young lady, medallion held high, but could not spot her. Curiously, where I had expected the 'hen-do' to be, there was a mangy looking fox, trotting invisibly around busy feet. It turned briefly back at me, as if I had called it, before going back to sniffing around the fishmongers.

I rubbed my eyes and looked over my shoulder back to the bar where I had just left. Nothing inside had changed, everyone there as I left them. Including that enchantress, impossibly back inside, a magician's reveal, staring back at me. I turned and pushed back inside, hesitating only briefly enough to twist my face at what drunken streetside delusion was still lingering over my shoulder. As I approached, the lady seemed to be evading me down winding cellar stairs. With hands trembling, I clutched her arm and stammered for the countless questions stalled at my lips.

The bar went black from a storm, and there now seemed to be a thick gray fog all around me. My once gentle softly painted beauty, now looked polarized in a terrifying blacklight. Her feet lifted off the floor, as she levitated above me and shrieked with an ungodly high-pitched scream. Her lungs screeched so loudly, I closed my eyes tight in fear that all the glass windows would explode. Her shrills shook the walls, killed the electricity and dropped me to my knees. And then, it was over. The lights were back on, the patrons continued to bustle about, I was left alone on the floor and she was gone.

The power glowed back to life, and the pub denizens seemed unphased. No one seemed to notice anything but the temporary power surge, resuming their banter. Some of them looked uncomfortably at me, the weird man on his knees in a bar. I was shivering a bit in disbelief before I glanced about for any sign of acknowledgement from the surrounding patrons on what devilry had just occurred. Everyone avoided eye contact, dismissing me as a drunk, except the barkeep who hovered glaringly above. An old gruff bald man with navy tattoos all along his bulldog arms, propping him up across the bar as he shook his head.

He walked around to help me to my stool, promptly pouring three shots of Irish whiskey between us, taking one for himself. "This will help." he muttered with coarse condolence. "Did you see… the…", I shuddered while clutching at my second shot glass. He cut me off quickly in a full-throated northside accent, "I saw nottin', I know nottin'. Best notta be asking questions when faery magic is about."

He began to pour me another shot, but I had to decline. "I really. must be. getting back to my hostel," working to string a sentence together. Upon rising, my knees buckled a bit, wary of what was waiting outside the pub's red door, and so I sat back down. "On second thought, do you have a room at the inn upstairs?"

The pug-faced man nodded, "Aye, should have, but we only let by the week. And we'll need a cash deposit," as he looked me up and down warily. I rifled immediately through my pockets to see what I had.

"I am not sure I have enough cash on me," as I uncrumpled some bills and sorted coins on the bartop. But the man quieted my nerves with a steady hand, as he put his finger down onto the one large medallion that stood out prominently amongst the pile. "Forget it, I'll just take tis 'ere coin off yer hands, and we'll call it square. Best I hold onto that anyways," he added before taking the chewing gum out of his mouth and using it to press the coin up on the back wall, nestled between a cluster of hanging polaroids, old cash bills, and other vintage trinkets.

I finished my last shot of whiskey and hoisted my backpack onto my shoulder, heading upstairs to my chambers. With my hand on the skinny white hallway door, I turned back to the barkeep for one last muttered attempt. "What just happened here", the most sincere of so many other questions fluttering about in my head.

Oddly anticipating them all, he shut me up with one simple reply. "Bad enough to try to grab one, but lad, you never, ever bargain with a banshee."

PART TWO

My whole life I have been plagued with bad sleep. If it wasn't anxiety nightmares, it was night terrors. And if it wasn't either of those, it was insomnia. However, that night, I slept uninterrupted in a peace I had not known since I was a small child. Making my way up to my rented room after an untrusted, psychedelic chain of evening events; I dozed off immediately. There was some hint of commotion and the roaring of what sounded like helicopters outside my window, along the Liffey River. Yet, despite all of their searchlights and patrolling, I dozed in my slumber and had just the most bizarre and soothing of dreams.

It is difficult for me now to recall the details, like any fading dream losing the buoyancy of its dreamworld logic. But I do remember that she was there with me, in all her fair faced beauty. She floated above me muted in dim light, dress and hair flowing about as if she was underwater. And she whispered the words to me that helped me feel safe and protected.

I melt to vapor. Sailing through dreams. Your face, my lost love's lure.
Dreams permit whispers. Love letters passed in secret. I conspire, for
you.
A bargain we've now made. Damned, though I be. Your burdens, I vow
to share.

Next day, I made my way down in the late morning to the bar and to the welcomed sight of a proper lunch carvery station being set up. Beasts and birds, roasted veg, some meat pies and coffee… ah, coffee. I set my laptop bag down at a table and my hands clutched plate and teacup with an eager gratitude. There was a bit of commotion at the windows as the lunch patrons hummed and gazed towards the obvious clustering of Garda cars, patrollers and a diving unit truck. It seemed to be the wrapping up of a crime scene, as barricades were being unlinked, and flashing cars sped away. I leaned an ear in to hear the gossips of my neighboring table, drowned out only a little by my own ravenous coffee slurping.

I heard a few different accounts, as you'd expect from the Irish among me, some wild embellishments and a whole lot of posturing about who's scoop had the inside track. Some people were reading the Times directly from their phones, some had claimed their second cousin is in the Irish Coast Guard, others had said they just walked out there to strike up a chat with the bored young patrolmen milling around. But the most shocking account seemed to come from the shivering lone survivor herself, who was delirious enough last night to talk to a camera crew in her very thick Geordie accent, before being whisked away by an ambulance. The exclusive was broadcast on the local news and went viral immediately.

The shattered young girl from Newcastle in her post traumatic state ranted and trembled about the death of her three friends. She showed disbelief in how the first one had fallen into the River Liffey, at the end of a long night out drinking. She recounted in horror how each of her friends followed to try to rescue the other. And she wailed deeply in guilt ridden remembrance to tell the reporter with the microphone, that the only reason she was alive was because she was too frozen with terror to offer any aid at all.

I shuddered at this retelling and watched the video on my phone in complete disbelief. I thought of the evening before, the events that I was so eagerly trying to dismiss and wash away with my hot coffee. I thought of the hen-do and the Newcastle girls dancing about. I remembered each of their faces, God rest their souls. I remembered the one girl on the video as one of them. But most of all, I remembered the white dressed girl that danced apart, tapping each one gently on the shoulder except for one. The lone survivor, the one that couldn't help but watch her friends drown that night.

I felt sick immediately and pushed my barely touched lunch plate away from me. I decided to skip my second coffee, and went straight to a cheeky mid-day Guinness. As I relocated to a barstool, I pulled up near to where I sat the evening past, and spotted that strange medallion, er, coin hanging there still, on the back wall straight across from me. I can't say why but it was this curious coin that reminded me more than anything else that last night was not just a dream. And more than any news story, or any squawking gossip, it was this coin's tale and her whispers of the open sea that I wanted to listen to most of all.

I shook that from my head and scrambled for a logical ballast position. The things I knew to be true, a way back to reality. I looked around to find the pug-faced gruff barkeep, but only saw a young skinny lad minding his iPhone from behind the bar. How much had I had to drink, had I taken something stronger, did someone slip me something? I could not demystify anything, not with the deepest of reasoning, so I went on to my third pint to see if more haziness would help.

For the most part, I found myself starry eyed of the image of that tragically captivating redhead. But each time I tried to remember her green glowing eyes, I was interrupted by the memory of her screaming spirit hovering above me in warning. And each time, I looked outside the window of this little pub, forgetting already the very horrific tragedy that befell those poor English girls, I could feel the odd lurking of an old-world Dublin, out there waiting, lost in time.

And through all this pondering, I finally snapped to attention in recalling what that wildling flower-crowned girl had said about my aunt and what she had offered me in exchange. I stood up to take the last swig of my stout, dropped a bill on the bar and hopped up the stairs to my room to call my mother back in the States. She was relieved to hear my voice and fell into her usual monologue about her day, my father, and other family gossip. All fairly common, everything in order. I kept asking about my father's sister, my aunt, to be sure there was nothing wrong, but she only shook it off and seemed unconcerned.

That evening, I spared one short thought about the banshee's bargain. Although my aunt seemed fine, I remembered the offering I was to make. Two names. Two names of my enemies written in ink and placed under a glass that I have sipped. And then what? She would be spared? At what cost? I shook my head at this foolishness and decided to stay another few nights at the inn, where I had slept so well for the first time in many years. I told myself that tomorrow I would take a break from my country wanderings and commit to Dublin for a few more weeks. Tomorrow I would troll through the freelancing job boards to see if I could get some billable consulting hours. It seemed time to get a bit more money in my pocket if I was going to be staying longer in the city.

And although I filled my schedule with some mindless but lucrative gigs, my focus often broke from the events that had passed. True to the harolds of that mysterious flower crowned girl, in two days time, I awoke to a text message from my mother, asking me to call her. She told me that my aunt had passed unexpectedly in the night, and that the funeral arrangements were being made for that week. I only spoke briefly with my father, and although he seemed to put on a brave tone, I could tell he was inconsolable.

The funeral was on a Thursday, and I regretted not being able to cut my travels short in time to pay my respects. I spoke to my cousins at length and sent them a mass card from a local parish here. I pressed forward feeling a little less certain about the natural order of the world and what I had seen a few days past. In the days that followed, I worked every day, drank every night, and prayed every morning for my family. Pondering deeply if I had truly invited a curse of death that I should've bargained against.

PART THREE

A week went by like this, while I sat at this bar, along with many other cafes scattered about town. I busied myself with billable hours, which I picked up easily from the job boards. Eventually, bringing in a bit of money and opting to extend my stay at the Ferryman Inn, I lingered longer in the city than I had intended. My ambitions to explore the West coast of Ireland and the Wild Atlantic Way was put on hold.

After filling my long days with billable hours and heavy pints, I often found myself sleeping at this inn like never had before. Swept away by some fevered fugue, I was haunted by the strangest of dreams. Running through the wilderness on starlight nights, naked like a feral wolf, and howling as one. The full moon rose over the ridges of the mighty Wicklow mountains, beautiful and chilling. I would call them nightmares except that I had never felt so serenely wild and at peace.

And of course, there were those nights I dreamed only of her. That sprite-like woodland woman, in bare muddy feet, and a frail white slip. Spinning me around the center of a circle of guests, all cheering us on and toasting our ceremony. I could never forget her wide kelly green eyes, glistening at me with the promise of forever. I would wake from these dreams, desperate and crying out as if I had lost that promise. And I was desperate to find her again. So continued my stay at the inn, weeks turning into months, and the winter winds stirring a frost along the river. Every night, I warmed myself by the pub's stone hearth, drinking hot whiskey and watching the door expectedly at every patron's arrival. But the strawberry haired girl with a crown of wild flowers, never came.

Until one day, a frail old man in his nineties with a large barnacled nose, came through the heavy red door, clutching his heavy wool coat. His trembling hands grasped at his first tall pale ale of the day as he took a high table on his, amidst the shouting masses. A gentleman out of time, wearing his Sunday's best, and putting his wool cap and cane at his side, as he sat dignified and upright while sipping his bitter beer. I tried not to stare, but caught myself fascinated with his stoically solitary figure, smugly content, like he had a secret. He remained dignified as he exchanged loud coughs with asthmatic gasps between his sips. And I finally turned to face him squarely from my seat at the bar, when I realized he was not alone.

She had been with him the entire time. Her arm slung around his shoulder, like his prized eldest daughter, bobbing her head cheerily between her shoulders to the beat of the music, and prodding him to dance along. She was smiling with kind interested eyes, as she warmed his arm with her soothing slender hand. Until she felt my stare, and locked eyes with mine, skittishly and in the same curious awe I shared with her. As I leaned a bit to stand, she tensed, as a deer would freeze on the approach of a hiker. She kissed her gentleman ward on the cheek and bid him farewell, before slipping deftly through the crowd away from me.

I rose to follow her, this spirit woman that lived in my dreams, that I had been waiting months to find. Unclear what I wanted from her, but only to see her eyes on my face again, adoring me. But as I took a few steps in her direction, she paused at the top of the top of the winding cellar stairs, finger tips sweeping the banister. She glared at me from across the crowded room and shook her head sternly side to side, mouthing the words 'no,' and warning me not to follow.

She glided down those stairs, fingertips now sweeping the railing like a tethered descending balloon. And she disappeared down below into the dark of the stone rathskeller bar. By reflex and without knowing why, I was moved to follow. But not before following an intuitive urge to duck, stealthily and unnoticed, behind the main bar to retrieve her gold medallion off the wall. I hastily peeled its sticky gum off the wall, longing to feel its possessing magic again, unsure if I was meant to return it to the girl in the white dress.

The patrons began to fade from my sight in rolling fog. The stairs in the corner of the room bent into a myopic tunnel ahead. And at every step down those stairs, the contrast of color grew dimmer, and my breath turned to cold mist.

There was no sign of the girl at first, or anyone at all in this abandoned cellar tavern. The room was a neat and tidy antique in itself, less kitschy than upstairs, like a staged roped off historical exhibit. There were leather books on the walls, a small Singer sewing machine in the corner, rickety wooden tables, and a smooth stone floor. And although the room was vacant, strangely enough, scattered red candles had been lit along the bookshelf walls. And a roaring center hearth fire had been neatly stoked, casting dancing shadows of people along the floors, and splashing warm orange light across an old wooden desk. The chair beside it seemed to be bowing for me to take a seat there.

I sat quietly by the cellar's hearth and before long, felt the touch of a soft slender hand on my shoulder. She pushed her finger against my chin, to warn me not to turn around to face her, as she whispered gently in my ear.

"You must not continue to see me, my love is gone, I seek no other. I cannot protect you from the curse you've stolen from me. But I will stay true to my word. Do you still remember our bargain? I have vowed to stay off the stalking scythe of Death from sweeping your loved ones."

I did remember her words but struggled to understand what riddle she was presenting to me. And before I was able to open my lips to ask, she pressed in closer, more sternly. And I saw her skin go pale and electric, like before, a wraith of hovering terrible warning.

"Listen to me now. Your father will die in three days' time. Write down three names of your enemies and leave them with me, under a glass your lips have touched, and your father will be absolved of your curse."

Horrified at her words, and the foreboding she offered, so much sterner and more chilling than the prophecy she had uttered before. I found myself standing up and facing her, as her feet touched the floor and the color returned radiantly to her high cheeks. I stepped away backwards, our hands interlaced, and pulling slowly apart, as she smiled a pouting farewell. And I turned to run terrified back up the staircase, the tunnel tightening into stairs, the cold white mist fading, and the sounds of the main hall's patrons all jeering loudly again.

I pushed through the crowd, dropping some money at my barseat, and scooping up my messenger bag for a fast retreat upstairs to my bedroom. Before putting my hand on the exit door to the upstairs inn, a thick hairy knuckled hand pressed against my chest. And I looked up to see the stout bald barkeep, looking at me expectedly. His other palm opened to me.

"Haven't you forgotten something? Best you give back that there coin, boyo." I surrendered the coin, without hesitation, and continued up to my room to call my mother. Asking after my father.

PART FOUR

This time, my mother was in tears on the phone, and my father had in fact fallen ill, admitted to the local hospital. And I told her I would be on tomorrow's flight from Dublin, home to New York.

The next morning, I waited with my backpack at the bar for my taxi to the airport. I sat somberly washing my nerves back with one last stout, pouring over a small piece of paper I had torn from a notebook. I thought harder this time about what the banshee had said and what she was asking of me. And although I could not fully submit to the superstition, I could not deny the paranormal crossroads I had encountered. So I decided, just in case, to search deeply for two names of my enemies. Whatever constituted an enemy, I had no idea. I thought hard about two names of people that had particularly gone out of their way to wrong me. Not knowing what would become of them or what I was trading.

If I was trading these lives for my father, I wondered if I was giving them a death sentence in return. Regardless of how my worst enemy had wronged me, it was a decision with consequence that made my stomach turn. I could only test my nerve, by trying to write the first name that came into my head. The name of a mean self-interested boss I once had, an old rival at a prior company, who had really gone out of her way to conspire against me and manager me out. I felt awful just thinking about it, even knowing writing her name as my enemy could not be anything more than a dark thought.

My taxi arrived outside the window, so I gave up on this naming game, and slung a rucksack over my shoulders. Standing up tall to chug my remaining pint, I folded that loose scrap of paper in half and left it under the empty glass. As I pushed outdoors to load up my luggage in the boot of the cab, I turned briefly back to glance through the window at the barstool I had just left. And although there was no one behind the bar at the time, now or when I had turned to leave, that small paper note I had left by my glass was nowhere to be seen.

True to my greatest fears, and to the sorrow of my family, my father did in fact pass from this world, not in two days, but in three. I spent the month back grieving with my mother and my two close sisters. It was a time of blurry confusion and just when I thought I would never feel ready to return to my own life, I received some news.

An old lost coworker had texted me his condolences, but had also asked if I had heard about the old boss we shared in common, from where we had worked before. She had apparently died unexpectedly just a few days ago. And quite violently he had added, in a head on collision, straight through the windshield and scattered across the highway. It would seem that her name, this one name, was worth one single day. And I wondered if two names may or may not have spared me the loss of my father. One name had bought him only one extra day on this earth. Still, it was one day I remembered fondly, sitting at his bedside at the hospital, reading him his favorite book.

Dead On Stats & Datasets, *a playfully paranoid sci-fi*

Sometimes the truth has set a collision course, ready to knock you on your ass like a box truck. And in the case of Arthur Slate, it was quite literally a box truck that knocked him over his head with an unexpected truth. His body laid askew across the pavement next to his bent bicycle, one wheel still spinning helplessly on its back. His forehead pooled crimson swirls into a knocked over cup of Starbucks mocha latte. In other contexts, the swirling reds and carmels could've been considered high art, curated alongside a Pollack collection. The bobbies were questioning the involved lorry driver, who was tearing his hair out in guilty disbelief. They were checking Arthur's cracked phone for any identification, and found a cycling tracker app, open and still scrolling through his 'Year in Review.' Milestones and achievements. Personal bests and year-over-years. The paramedics futilely scrambled to stabilize the poor and careless Arthur, as he began gasping to mutter something through the oxygen mask, just before flatlining, "I just... I just... needed to get to a meeting. Can you ask if I got the promotion?"

***

Arthur woke up on a cold metal slab to disorienting surroundings. A neat, gaunt man in silver scrubs was looming over him, fiddling with a holographic tablet hovering at his side. The room was washed with white light that obscured the seams of the walls. Strange barnacle encrusted vacuum tubes wove messy tripping hazards all across the floor.

"Mr. Arthur Slate. Checked in. Pronounced dead, on the galactic timestamp of... well you don't care. You lot never can grasp true time anyways...' the gaunt man seemed to be talking to himself before returning his eye gaze. 'Welcome my friend! 'OH NO!' You're probably thinking! 'IT'S ALL SO SUDDEN, THIS CAN'T BE HAPPENING!' Etcetera, etcetera." Then leaning closer to Arthur's frozen face, with an honest appeal, "Look here, sunshine, could we just get past all that? We've all heard it a million times before. And frankly, it's a bit cliche, don't you reckon?"

Arthurs mouth was intubated, but his thoughts seemed to be going to a dialogue screen. "Hmm, am I joking? Fraid not, chap. You really are dead." The thin man dismissed Arthur's frantic queries, flipping distractedly through his tablet.

"Is this heaven, did you just ask? Hahaha, that's very good. Yeah, sure, that's what this is. Heaven, he asks! My, my, my, that one never gets old." Then clearing his throat for a bit more tact, "Um, I mean, no. Fraid not on that one too, buckeroo. So sorry. This is, um, well, how should I explain?"

Arthur sent another message regarding his pending promotion.

"Oh well, now you're talking! That one I CAN answer. Let's see here.. flipping, flipping, filtering probability variances, collapsing to your most probable reality. Ah! There it is... Nope. Sorry mate, that one went to... let me see, right, a man named Steve." The thin man pushed the word out like it hurt his bottom teeth. "A terribly boring bloke, it seems. But don't worry, he'll only last about two years before getting sacked. Don't think you would've lasted much longer either. Oh, and the stress of it all gives him a deadly brain aneurysm the year after. Will you look at that? Guess that's why they call it the blues, eh? So you see, you didn't miss out on much, did you, old sport?" suggested the poised man, attempting to build some rapport.

Arthur kept trying to push words past his taped up mouth tubes, and only managed to send incomplete questions, mostly stutterings regarding the scaley vacuum tubes plugged into his arms, legs and torso.

"But, but, but... spit it out, meatbag!" mocked the man before composing himself. "Sorry, I'm only messing about. You're not supposed to see all those tubes, here we go." With a finger swipe, all the medical apparatus dissolved, pixelated into thin air. And although Arthur couldn't see them, he sort of suspected they were still there.

Arthur accepted that this was not the pearly gates of heaven. But it still followed that he was very much dead. The cold stainless steel table made him feel like he was in a hospital. But everything else seemed to scream 'spacecraft!' God, he pleaded, hoping he hadn't been abducted by some twisted extraterrestrials. Curiously, he found himself worrying mostly about the 'bum play and probings' for which aliens had had such a devious reputation.

"Aliens? Oh god, no, nothing like THAT." Interrupted the looming, dead-eyed attendant. "Although, I suppose I'm not technically human, despite how I'm being projected. As to where you are, I suppose the most relatable thing to say is, welcome back to the mainframe. And before you ask, I'm not going to teach you kung fu or be feeding you any red pills. Heard that all before."

Arthur sighed the word 'figures' and was far less panicked than he should be, given his grim situation.

"Figures, indeed. But we'll get to those later. Now, since you've had a chance to relax and settle in, let me just get these nasty little legal details out of the way. Please pay attention, this is the last time I'm going to read this:

"Waiver and Disclaimer: you one, Arthur Slate, have been reacquired per your unique source entity's contract, for an unspecified (albeit brief) period of interstitial existence, during which time your incarnations cache will be reappropriated for data mining by the Bureau of Galactic Data Extraction."

Arthur started to mumble wildly, but the thin man swiped and deleted his floating text messages, as he continued reading a bit louder.

"Per your non-disclosure agreement, the B.G.D.E. (I know, shite name to be fair), *will have exclusive rights to all statistics, lifetime interactions, causal inactions, observations, and not excluding subjective opinions and self-formulated world views (no matter how inconsequential or ridiculous, I should add). After extraction, your data memories and life cache will be wiped clean, stripped to source code and...* blah, blah,

blah… *back into the nearest existential redistribution center for reboot version number…"*

His eyes fluttered the open document, puzzled at first, "Hmm, it's supposed to list the next gen version here. Oh well, regardless, just need your little thumbprint on the screen to acknowledge," snatching Arthur's thumb and doing it for him, he waited for a green progress bar to read 1%. "And away… we… go…"

If Arthur could gulp audibly, he would've. He was stuck on the latter sentence about being wiped shortly and tried to whimper a bit. That was audible.

"Now, now, champ, it's not as bad as you make it sound, you're one of the good ones. I mean look at all this gorgeous data! You've lived a busy life, mate. And oh my lord, see all this here," the man swung the floating screen around to show Arthur a smattering confusion of diagrams and charts. "The self-obsessive reflections, you've curated, albeit a bit indulgent, this stuff is like gold dust! No, no, trust me, we need you to go back in. Mine us more gold like this! Probably with a different country origin, however. Different race, gender, priviledge, etcetera etcetera, you understand."

Arthur's chin was quivering now at the prospect of having to start all over, wondering if he'd have to begin as a baby again. Would he retain anything? And if not, was he even the same person? More importantly, what if he rolled a really shitty family, a shitty town, a shitty body? A shitty life? He liked who he was now, and he didn't want to roll dice on something different.

"Listen, I can see you're a little upset. But can you keep a secret?" The thin man glanced around like a kid showing off his hidden toys, but his smugly wide-eyed grin just made him look creepier. "We have some time to pass, you want to play a little game, something to take your mind off things? I'm really not supposed to, but what the hell! Afterall, this is my last week in this grueling reprocessing division. You see, I have been promoted," he stood up straight, pulling back his shoulders, proudly expecting Arthur's overjoyed admiration. But Arthur held his blank, dumbfounded stare. The tall attendant dropped his shoulders back down, and tried again.

"So, I don't mean to brag, but you just happen to be looking at the new SENIOR analyst to the Junior Deputy Administrator for the Data Overflow Department! You know! Reporting to the Executive Ministry at the Bureau of Archives for Abstract Thoughts!! CAN YOU BELIEVE IT?!"

Still nothing from Arthur, as the perturbed slim analyst, returned his fingers to screen tapping.

"Well, trust me, it's a really big deal, all the idiots down here are supremely jealous. But, listen, my point is… what was my… Oh yes, I'm mostly checked out, we could have a little fun while we wait. There is this little game I've been cooking up with the data slices we take from you body dwelling folk. It's part of what got me noticed from the higher ups, who were most impressed by my…"

Arthur was rolling his eyes but shrugged a sign he was willing to listen.

"Right, nevermind that now. What do you know about Spotlight Reels?!" the lanky fellow blurted excitedly like a gameshow host. "It's like a fun fact trivia game. I got the idea from your last world. You know how all those apps like Spotify give you end of the year statistics, sort of a 'your year in review' type of thing? Well, I've found a clever way to do that with all this life data we're extracting, all assembled in neat and engaging little slide cards. Except this time, they're about your *whole* life! Every milestone, missed opportunity, personal bests and year over years. That type of thing. Exciting, right? I mean, who doesn't love hearing about themselves? The boys upstairs are clearly very impressed with my work, if I do say. Well, what do you think? You up for it, cowboy?"

PART TWO

The hollow-framed man busily click-dragged a few windows and then grabbed all the little tiles and threw them onto a spinning 3D axis that expanded over Arthur's head. A title card emerged at the front of the stack simply reading, 'Arthur's Life in Review'.

"Ok kiddo, we're set to go, let me just filter some of the cosmic events you won't care about, maybe just skim through some of the boring details first. This first section is called 'Fun with Numbers'.

"Arthur Slate, male human incarnation, aged thirty-six at time of death. Height, top fourteen percentile. Health and bodyweight twenty-three percentile. Facial symmetry, nine percentile, way to go, you handsome stud! Self-esteem, however, forty-two percentile. So you probably can't take a compliment.

"Let's see, total minutes awake, total time sleeping, eating, shagging, all pretty standard. Ah, 499,999,991 breaths taken! Shame, that, only nine breaths away from a round number. Should've filed that under 'missed opportunities'. Number of hours pondering unknowable questions, ugh, too many. What else, total calories consumed, yuck, total burned, admirable, steps taken, what am I, your fitbit… doot doot doot...

"Ah, here we go, percent of your time talking in a conversation, seventy-one. Percent of time listening to others, twenty-nine. Tsk tsk! But look at here, you gave more than you received! That's something. Over twenty years of gift-giving, bar rounds and dinner tabs, you spent 452,000 pounds, and received back about 245,000! Perhaps your gravestone will read, 'consistently tipped over 25%'. I'm kidding, of course. Come on, no one said we can't have fun here.

"OK, moving on, years of being remembered after death: twelve. Hey, that's good for someone with no offspring! I'd be happy with that. Percent chance of becoming famous if death had not occurred, ew, you don't want to know that one, chap. It was high.

"Total near death experiences, eleven. The worst one was… oh you know this one, scary wasn't that? Number of times you shirked responsibility, twelve million and eleven, only 14% of which had a life impacting effect. No seriously, it's written right there. Oh, the things we can get away with, eh?

"Ready to move on? It gets more fun from here. The next section, I've titled: 'Unique about you.' A shameless appeal to your ego, I know. Let's find out what you do more than anyone else. Sound good, sport? Top 5% for self-reflection, not bad. Top 1% for self-obsession, unsurprising. Most frequent thought outside yourself, oh there it is, boobs, naturally. Moving swiftly onwards.

"Most consumed meal is french fries, really mate? Not going to get many ladies that way. Favorite curse word is fuck, naturally. Where's the unique stuff, this needs some tweaking. Ah, there we go! You use the word 'tit' more cleverly than any of your peers, like 'going tits up to a party' or 'that fellow's a bit of tit.' Also, you said the word 'preposterous' more than any other living person in history. You find that hard to believe? Would you go so far as to describe it as impossible, ridiculous, ludicrous? Or some… other… word?

"You're not impressed, I can tell. How about this: your best day ever was November 14th at age thirty-one. Doesn't list why, hmm, just some random balance of feel good chemicals swirling about your brain, I guess. Also, did you know, you've never touched your own left pinky toe? Not once. You came really close on a beach in Portugal, and we all almost lost our minds. What a fun day at the office that was."

The peculiar thin man seemed miles away thinking of better days, before breaking his daze, and noticing Arthur's growing impatience.

"Look, is this stuff not interesting to you? I suppose there's all sorts of majestic events I could serve up, things so rare and beautiful that happened only to you at a quantum level. Nanosecond, once-in-a-galactic age events so fragile, so unique, they could not be described in words. And you alone witnessed them, albeit only on a subconscious level. But let me guess, you want to know more about love. So triflingly predictable, but fine, here you go.

"Soul mates encountered and snubbed. Zero. God that's depressing. What's that? No, no, soul mates do exist, it's not just a myth. It's just, uh, a bit uncommon. And more commonly, it's true when they say, there really is someone for everyone. Just, um, for your specs, I'm afraid not you. Saawwry."

Trying to break the awkward silence with some better news, "Well, hmm, how about, adequate marriage candidates, previously dated? Four. And the best optimal candidate was, nope, it wasn't Kerry. It was Amy. Surprising, I agree, she was a nutjob. Yep, that would've guaranteed happiness, or at least, minimized unhappiness. Shame.

"Speaking of, here's the section I mentioned called, 'Missed Opportunities.' It's my absolute favorite. Like did you know, your whole life, you had undiagnosed dyslexia? Very mild, but it would've served you to have known that. Also, undiagnosed sleep apnea. My god, did you think it was normal to feel that tired every morning? What else do we have here? Four undetected malignant tumors that miraculously ate themselves, not that interesting. Oh and remember how you kept getting that skin rash every winter? Peanut allergy. Yup, easily fixed if you had looked into it.

"Also, you weren't, as you often claimed, suffering from ADHD, but you did pick probably the lowest 40% of professions for your IQ and general aptitudes. So you see, you were just bored your whole life. Finance? Honestly, what were you thinking? The top profession you should've chosen? Right, that's here... it is... heating and plumbing contractor. I'm serious, it's right here, you would've created an empire, you had a gift.

Arthur was caught wondering why the gaunt man thought this smattering of 'too little, too late' truth bombs could pass for trivia. He was filled only with a sickening sense of existential helplessness.

"OK, your gray-green skin suggests this is overload. Maybe we'll take the focus off you, I can see how trifle upsetting. Speaking of upsetting, the next section is called 'IS THAT REALLY HOW THINGS WORKED?' Basically a list of surprising truths about the society you just left. We've only time to outline a few. But there will be time at the end of questions. Let's tear through these at pace, shall we?

"So, the world you just left was all driven by profits and debt. The entire economy is built on debt creation. Everything from construction to manufacturing, to soybean farming and veganism is propped up by a quickly depleting world oil reserve. All war was actually necessary to prop up domestic manufacturing. All business and trade is driven by the profit devices of some stock market algorithms. Those were emergent, not programmed, incidentally. That's right, no evil AI overlords, just a sophisticated program adapting for its own survival. Bonkers, right?

The pale tight-lipped man continued to droll on, speeding up slightly with the air of a stand-up comic bombing, and flipping desperately through his notes for the 'good stuff.'

"Also, there was a 'deep state' responsible for distracting and dumbing down the masses, inventing everything from mobile phones to Netflix. Bigfoot wasn't real, but the Loch Ness monster was. The moon landing was not faked, duh, but it is hollow. You wouldn't believe what's inside, but it's much more mind-blowing than just a survival bunker for billionaires. UFOs were mostly fake, but there was that one contact made, I think they gave you guys 'plastics', as a grossly misunderstood practical joke. Whoopsy.

"Final few tidbits here, champ. The happiest period in civilization was not in fact America in the 'Eighties', but a decade in eighth century Baghdad. Oh, you think you've been to a wild, late-night rave? Those chaps could part-tay! Buddhism was the only correct religion, although I hear Jesus and Muhammad were fairly nice blokes too. Oh and looky here, the FBI definitely did kill JFK. Wow. And lastly, a global killing asteroid is due for cataclysmic collision with your Earth in 2176. Phew, got through that. How you feeling?"

Arthur blinked slowly, not knowing how to react. Did this unimaginative analyst think this passed for entertainment? Did he think they were going to slap each other's backs and laugh off the absurdity of the world he had just departed?

"Well, happy camper, the good news is we're almost wrapped up here. And you're going to love our final segment. It's our speed round called, 'Questions from the Data Host.' That's you. Basically, handing it over to you for questions. Anything and everything you've ever wondered. And please surprise me. You wouldn't believe how many people just want to know if there's an afterlife after all these bloody reincarnations. Oh. That was your first question, wasn't it?"

PART THREE

Arthur decided not to ask about that, and quickly became overwhelmed with the opportunity at hand. There he was at the end of his life, or one of them. And he was offered up on a silver platter the chance to know anything. To understand everything. To have the thing kings, philosophers, stargazers, and data marketers have sought for all of civilization… the truth. And while racking his brain to come up with his first question, the only thought that persisted was how he wished he had painted more.

"Marvelous. I suppose you'd like to hear more about if you had worked harder to become a painter?" The cynical man said with feigned interest. "I thought we already covered professions, but very well. It would've been your nineteenth best profession. Certainly no plumbing destiny, I'll tell you that. But you would've found decent enough purpose, some peace of mind, despite all the 'suffering for my art' rubbish. And you would've had an adequate talent to make some impressions in small circles, in this hypothetical situation, that is. Would you like to see a catalogue of your highest rated works?

And then something occurred to Arthur, something he didn't think the gaunt man would anticipate.

"Sorry, you'd like me to pick your 'best' painting? How do you mean, 'best'? I have the aggregate ratings here, as I said. Or do you mean, best selling paintings? I suppose I could model that probability too. Or do you mean, the ones you would've been most likely to put in your portfolio based on market appeal? Or do you want me to calculate the total minute duration of impression gaze, for a popularity rating?

There it was, Arthur thought. This poor little mole of a data-miner, had no actual opinions of his own. He could only size something based on facts. He had no intuition, no preferences, no original opinions of his own. Arthur pressed him further to simply pull any painting that he liked, anything he favored, and not to overthink it. Reluctantly, this suddenly unsure of himself analyst picked an image, albeit rather flippantly, and expanded it to a stunning high resolution hovering above them.

Arthur muffled a gasp at the gripping palette of rookwood reds, pumpkin spice, & burnt sienna. All swirling into a familiar, yet surreal, asymmetrical country landscape. He recognized this from a childhood dream. It was an old beautiful capture of a long forgotten family lakehouse on a crisp, autumn saturated day. And Arthur began to weep at its convergence of long sunset shadows and its notion of waning innocence. Arthur asked for his right hand to be uncuffed so he could zoom in on his masterpiece. And then he returned his attention to his confused guardian for the next round of his questions.

"What do I think of it? I'm not clear why that matters. Um, I suppose I think it would've sold for 350,000 pounds sterling. And it could've been valued even higher at..." Arthur interrupted him, repeating his question. So the man started again.

"Well I suppose I think it was twenty-three percent of your brain's creative expression center, and if you really tried harder...." Arthur glared at him, signaling a variation on his question. "Oh all right," snapped the thin man, "What do I see in it? You could've just asked that. I suppose, I see, um. I suppose it makes me feel, hmm. I feel. I feel... nothing." The man appeared betrayed by his own vacant thoughts.

Arthur probed deeper now, asking him how he was going to handle his job working for the Bureau of Abstract Thinking, or whatever? Especially since it seemed he couldn't form any abstract thoughts of his own. It seemed these beings, or programs, or hallucinations, didn't have any creative capacity at all. And Arthur asked his unraveling attendant if he was feeling overwhelmed at all by this new approaching responsibility. Afterall, it seemed like a big job to interpret such complex datasets as subjective thoughts.

At that, the thin man broke down weeping and put a hand out blindly to ask for a moment to compose himself. "It's just that, I have worked so hard to get this promotion and I can't even muster a true emotion about it. I honestly have been so busy following this career path, I haven't had time to process how I feel about it. Only this looming notion that I'm faking my way upwards, that no one will take a fraud like me seriously. I'm sorry, I need to go use the bathroom, this is so embarrassing." At that, the broken little analyst departed flustered, hands over his quivering eyes.

And so Arthur got to work with his unbound hand, quickly swiveling the tablet over and surveying the unlocked control screen. It was a dizzying smattering of windows and meters, but his confusion started to wane as the advanced interface seemed to be calibrating to his language and preferences on its own. Arthur quickly spotted what he was looking for.

A flashing file link read, 'Requisition Order', he clicked open and quickly found the delete option. 'Reload to prior save point?', the prompt appeared. Arthur assumed this meant, back to where his body was back on Earth. Yes, he clicked. 'Are you sure, all progress unsaved will be lost?' Yes!!

'Delete cache of pending data upload? Hell yes. Arthur wanted no record of himself here. Unsync backup profile? Arthur, hovered over the prompt, desperately hoping this meant they couldn't recall him. Unless it meant he was erasing himself from existence entirely. The notion lingered and would've disturbed him deeply if he had had more time to dwell on it. Screw it. He clicked the prompt 'Yes,' and let out a sigh of relief. 'Unsynced, new profile refreshed, rebooting now.'

Arthur braced himself for the countdown, but then noticed one last flashing prompt. 'Warning, last chance to modify profile skills and behaviors.' Wait, what? Arthur hadn't realized he could, er, modify himself. He scanned furiously across digital dials and scales, as the progress bar hit 87%. Spotting a box called 'IQ & Self-confidence,' he quickly jacked the meter to the top of the scale. But then, he thought better of the consequences of being too smart. He panicked and tried to set it back to where it was, but couldn't remember. He made his best guess and hoped it was at least one notch higher.

Frantically scanning around the dials, Arthur felt the pressure to change something, anything, as the countdown ticked on. So many attunements he would've loved to make, but he imagined the mess of personality soup that could follow. Also, the instrument panel was just so busily inscrutable. And there simply was no time. But as the progress bar hit 99%, Arthur's eye caught one last category among the cluttered dashboard of meters. It was marked 'Charisma', and although he was sure there was no time left, Arthur reached for its twisting knob. Clockwise? He wasn't sure which was higher. As he pondered if one could have too much appeal, the reboot sequence finished and his body was dissolved in brilliant white light.

The gaunt man returned from the loo, red eyed, feeling silly but washed with relief, "Ah, Arthur, you have no idea how much I needed that. Arthur?" He slowly approached the barren steel slab table and glanced suspiciously at his control station. Holding his breath, he scanned to retrieve Arthur's profile but found nothing. "Yikes. This will not go over well," he muttered amused to himself. "But I suppose the chaps upstairs can't be mad about what they don't know." He quickly doctored a false report about a failed recall, that would likely confuse his replacement, but not look too suspicious. "Somebody else's problem now." the man shrugged before sparing a parting thought, "Arthur, it was a pleasure, I hope you make the most of your last go-round."

***

Arthur awoke back on the pavement to the resuscitations of the attending paramedic. When his eyes opened, the woman in a tight ponytail and ambulance shirt smiled, "You're going to be ok, handsome. Never mind all that blood beside you, looks worse than it is, just a bad bump really."

Arthur had no time to marvel at the red, wet fresco he had unwittingly laid. He instead fixed on his gaze on the prettiest flecks of green ever to sparkle in a woman's eyes. As the paramedic leaned in closely to verify there was no concussion, he also noticed a warm blush in her cheeks and decided to flash his smile to say, "This may sound preposterous, but I think you might just be an angel."

New Phone, Who Dis? *an optimistic alien contact*

PART ONE - Look, before we start rolling, you have to promise again you won't edit me as some lunatic conspiracy theorist. I've had enough trouble with alien invasion fanatics, new age cults camping outside my house. I only want to present the facts and get back to teaching. Life was so much simpler before all this. God, and so messy since this year, when all the records got declassified. Are we rolling? OK, well I suppose I should introduce myself.

My name's Dr. Emily Harper, I'm a tenured professor at Stanford, in the field of linguistics. Yes, I've worked with SETI before, consulting on some of their signal collection and analysis programs, code breaking basically. I mean, I'm a nerd at heart, I love those guys, it's a refreshing break, creating new languages, instead of studying old ones. And they had some shit hot tech! Sorry, I'm still a bit nervous. Tech that was making even the NSA jealous. But no, I had never worked with NASA before, certainly never dreamed I'd be contacted by their project team for the 2nd James Webb Telescope. That was an exciting phone call! I had only read about their launch in the news, but let's just say my inner space geek was fangirling pretty hard.

You have to understand, this was an exciting time for everyone across the world. It was the 50's! You know, the 2050's, stop it, I'm not that old. The Age of Complacency! Sorry, cut that, I don't want to sound cynical. You know, the Age of Autonomy, we had passed the crawling stages, the information age, the age of assistance. Most country's AI had reached general cognition, but not super intelligence or sentience, certainly not the 'singularity' that was predicted. We got that under better control quicker than expected. But we did have a monster of a powerhouse at our fingertips, general cognition, solving all our world's problems. You've read the stories, everything self-governing: self-building cities, self-governing construction sites, self-governing companies, households, lifestyles and wellness. We got pretty lazy as humans for a while. I say that with love, believe me, we all enjoyed the fruits of a newly automated world. It's just, we seemed to forget ourselves a bit.

Where was I? Solving our world's problems. Right, we were so busy with our attention turned inward, we stopped thinking about looking, you know, up. We used to dream of colonizing Mars for crying out loud, building a highway of space stations to the asteroid belt! Where were the dreamers and the futurists? So when I read about programs like SETI, NASA getting funded again, I was giddy. Making the biggest news waves, the funding for a new James Webb Space Telescope. If you know your history, this was the big one in the 2020's, replacing the Hubble. I was just a toddler, but I've been told we needed this, a reason to dream, afraid of germs, afraid of each other, afraid of annihilation. Hovering in low orbit with these majestic golden mirrors, the 'James Webb' was a beacon of hope, sending us back stunningly detailed images of the observable universe, light captured that was thirteen billion years old, back to the dawn of creation. They were gorgeous and chilling for the time, beautifully high definition, swirling palettes of galaxies and rippling gas clouds, like dynamic NFT artwork.

Is this OK so far? I don't need a break, but I know you're eager to get to the discovery. Let me just wrap this up. Remember again, we went into the next two decades still fearful of the artificial intelligence 'singularity', where we lost control of this dragon, like Prometheus chucking fire around a dry forest. Meanwhile, NASA was collecting all this interstellar data and pictures, they only lacked the resources to analyze the billions of tiny point pixels of stars and nebulae, sorting out which ones could have earth-like planets.

Oh right, I should explain that, 'seeing' exoplanets is pretty hard outside our solar system, they're too small and swallowed up by the immense light of the nearest star. It's like measuring a spec of dust wedged deep into one glowing pixel of a gigantic IMAX screen. Except you know, billions of miles away. But we have some clever tricks, you know, we could take photos and compare them, if the slight dimming implied an exoplanet eclipsing its own star. Or we can detect small wobbles in the star, implying what tiny gravity forces are tugging at it. So 'measuring' exoplanets, opposed to 'seeing' them, was an incredibly slow and tedious way to do detective work. But hey, you're interviewing some really smart astronomers after me, so let's move on.

The point here is mapping out the universe, surprise surprise, was hard. Call it fractal, the closer you look, the more infinitely complex it gets. We needed higher resolutions, we needed swarms of multi-angle feeds, the 'before and after shots' weren't good enough. And of course we needed incredible processing power to analyze it all. And all our AI resources were busy, turned inwards, solving our 'real world' problems, energy crisis, climate change, economic collapse. You name it, we had a queue and space programs weren't a priority. But once all that dust settled, like I said, it was the 50's, we were hitting the bottom of our to-do list, maybe we were getting bored, so imagination and innovation started to get, um, fashionable again.

Enter James Webb 2.0, aka Spiderman, thirty years after the original. It was a new beacon of hope in the scientific community. It represented everything to us, a chance to build and study new fields again, it meant we had cleared the smaller worries, and our gazes returned to the stars. It was a beautiful, well funded project, so much bigger, so much more powerful. It operated analogously the way original search engines like Google used spider programs, trillions of feeler programs bouncing around the galaxy, returning mountains of data, video feeds and in 3D! Or 4D even, if you count the age of the light. Most importantly, Webb 2.0 would be powered by the slickest, state-of-the art AI for analysis at quantum scales of speed and detail, simultaneously in space and at the control station, the intelligence they affectionately named MARVIN.

PART TWO

MARVIN not only mapped our entire galaxy in the first week, and three more in the following weeks, but a list of hundreds of thousands, millions, of habitable earth-like planets. Without being asked, it... er, they, MARVIN, developed this neat little quality score, the highest probable planets we could send probes to, maybe even communicate with, if we were rolling dice for sentient life. Imagine our surprise when they told us not to even bother with the list they just created. Instead, suggesting we focus all our focus on one star system, one small planet near the Pillars of Creation gas clouds, roughly 7000 light years away! Not exactly a close prospect for sending probes or unmanned terraforming missions. When we asked MARVIN why, they said, and this always gives me chills, because it's already sending us a signal waiting for our response.

Hold on, quick sip of water. Sorry, putting my phone to vibrate, my sister's family is in town. Let's keep rolling, this is where it gets exciting, when I got the call that upturned my life. SETI had recommended me to NASA, and before you know it, I was on a military escort helicopter, fully badged and signing all sorts of NDAs, en route to some underground bunker. You've seen the movies. Exactly like that. War Games, Contact, The Day the Earth Stood Still, none of these classics could've prepared me for what came next. The briefing went like this: we were getting a broadcast that turned out to be a series of primers from something, well, sentient. The first primer was just blinking light, again, that signal would've been 7000 years old. Exciting, but hardly a chance for a dialogue. But then MARVIN decrypted it and found the next cipher, a key used to connect to some subspace transmission. That science is its own story, believe me. But now the broadcast was real time! Crazy, I know.

No one cared how excited I was, there was no time. The staff hurried to catch me up on their current problem. It's alien, it's real-time, they're trying to learn our language, for a chat, yes with aliens, get over it, get onboard. That type of tone. I was outside my field, clearance level and all, but I still couldn't help asking questions. LInguists are curious. While the dIrectors and colonel's were scurrying about, I scratched around for more theories, fast asides to the real project heroes, the young post-grad analysts, all restraining their inner geek-outs. My people! One of these enthusiastic nerds, let's call him Carl, adorably spazzy and over-caffeinated, he had the best theories to share. He named the lifeform, Kwatz, some old sci-fi reference, an exclamation that some superintelligence used to poke fun at dumb questions from dumb humans. This described its playful tone pretty well. No one knew whether it was one individual, a collective civilization, or an AI itself. Carl seemed convinced Kwatz was disembodied, maybe digital, thousands of years old, maybe immortal, and hyper-intelligent - too intelligent for them to find any common ground for communication.

Of course, in all the quiet watercooler whispers, there was that elephant in the room. Was this intelligence waving hello, acting curious, or prepping the invasion plans? I'll leave it to the other scientists to explain all the 'dark forest' jitters. Safe to say, there was a resounding regret in the room that we had broadcasted our huddled location in the galaxy at all. But the bell had been rung, so the powers in charge kept us plowing forward. Carl had told me they followed all Kwatz's instructions to create dozens more ciphers, uploading mountains of our information, languages, art, pop culture, wikipedia - everything. Kwatz was trying to learn our language from scratch, but it seemed like overkill for such slow moving progress. Kwatz always seemed confused by our early attempts, "greetings from the people of earth, we bring tidings of peace." That kind of empty nonsense. Barely using any of our language, Kwatz would send back bleeps and blurts that somehow seemed sarcastic. Playful or just patronizing, Kwatz was starting to test everyone's patience.

Look, credit goes to the team for getting us this far, but it was clear they had no idea how to make first contact. It was Carl and I that aligned here, impressing that Kwatz wasn't being obtuse or withholding, they just didn't know where to start. Firstly, they had the intel but not the context, for all we knew this 'being' was some type of light energy that had no real concept of shapes and forms, probably a vastly different concept of time. So it could use words like 'small' or 'before', or 'bring' or 'peace', but not really comprehend them. Also something seemed familiar in how Kwatz was holding back, like they didn't want to embarrass us. The way you'd contact a tribe of apes in the wild, not trying to use your language, wary of mimicking theirs, so as not to offend. Just making small gestures, bowing, submitting.

But we kept pushing and encouraging Kwatz, and *they* started sending some bizarre attempts. The most intriguing of them came in the form of haikus, chinese proverbs or zen-like koans, like 'listen for the sound of one hand clapping.' Fascinating, I thought, so did Carl. Nobody else saw this as progress. Kwatz even sent us what felt like an 8,000 page Russian war and romance novel. Whether it was generative AI or not, it kept a team of analysts busy for a month, and Carl seemed to really enjoy it. Powerfully written, if not concise, but the subtext of the whole novel seemed to be that Kwatz was simply trying to tell us they were lonely.

It was then Carl and I decided we needed to wipe the white board clean, we were coming at this problem from too many angles. And it was a text message from my thirteen year old nephew that changed my entire approach.

PART THREE

By the way, you know Kwatz's novel got submitted for publication, right? Just after the declassification, Carl's got a whole series of video essays praising it, ready to drop on his channel. It should be out this spring, I recommend the abridged version, though. Right, so my nephew's text message. My sister has raised a truly gifted young man, the apple of my eye. He got his first mobile device recently, with restrictions, because you know, he's got amazing, responsible parents. I was so happy when 'direct messaging' came back en vogue. God, don't get me started about blackholes technology had led us down prior. All the roll-backs to 'retro tech' were joyfully accepted, but the intimacy of a private 'dm' exchange is what I missed the most. And I was flattered my nephew wasn't too cool to text his aunt regularly. But the initial sessions were, say, primitive at best. A typical exchange:

>*Him: Sup.*
>*Me: hey hey hey, how's school? Tell me everything, I hear you aced your English exam, you know that makes a language geek like me so happy!*
>*Him: yeah, thx.*
>*Me: so what's been going on over there, I'm so excited to visit you, are you making big summer plans yet?*
>*Him: yeah, sort of. Bored.*

Quick aside, this is not how our conversations go in person. He's brilliant, high vocabulary, warm and engaging. But with this new form of communication, I got the feeling he was starting from zero on expressing himself, you know, digitally. You see where this is going? Eureka! This is what Kwatz needed, a simple interface, an easy way to start learning dialogue. If we could meet in person around a fire, like first contact between tribes, it would go faster, but this is what we were working with. So Carl and I briefed the team and launched a brand new project called 'DM ME'.

It didn't take long to copy a simple text format interface, and put our AI to work, teaching Kwatz through millions of iterative conversations, all in the style of a teenager. Kwatz seemed to immediately grasp the exercise. After some clunky starts, again with the russian novels or scattered mosaics of emojis, I'll spare you the details, we got to a baseline. We rebooted the whole conversation and started like it was our first. It was time for a real human test. As the generals quibbled about who should lead the exchange, it was Carl who quickly stood up for me, citing all the bombed attempts before I arrived. We had a linguist on the staff now, afterall, common sense. So I sat down at the control station's desk, the large bubble screen overhead on 16 screens, with hundreds of the world's best minds hovering around me in anticipation, as I typed, 'Sup'.

>*Me: 'sup.*
>*Kwatz: 'sup.*
>*Me: you good?*
>*Kwatz: naw.*
>*Me: sup???*
>*Kwatz: bored.*
>*Me: same.*

Naturally, it started the way I had expected, based on my experience with another young angsty teen, feeling his way through the dark. It was like a screenshot my nephew shared in confidence with me once asking for help, trying to text a girl he liked at school for the first time. Uncertain, reserved, no game. Ha, maybe cut this, everyone has a wobbly start flirting. Some overzealous colonels told me to ask, 'do you want to be friends,' but I shrugged him off. This was going to take some time.

In fact, Carl had the best idea, to completely treat this like a real life text exchange, to act like I had other things going on, take long breaks, appear distracted, put the onus on Katz to drive things. Kwatz probably also had better things to be doing, a brain maybe bigger than a planet, busy contemplating realities across dimensions, entertaining themselves with complex quantum puzzles, whatever cosmic super entities do for fun. Funny enough, they seemed to be enjoying this game just fine.

The dialogue went on for several days, but as you may already know by now, ended quite abruptly. And I think this is the exchange you've been waiting for, so let me just read some of it out:

>*Kwatz: hey again.*
>*Me: 'ello.*
>*Kwatz: whatcha up to?*
>*Me: kinda bored.*
>*Kwatz: already? aren't you early?*
>*Me: ???*
>*Kwatz: you know, plenty to do there, early planet.*
>*Me: oh i see. naw, been here a while, million years or so.*
>*Kwatz: that's nothing.*
>*Me: well, 12,000 years talking, million years walking ;)*
>*Kwatz: haha.*
>*Me: you good? Kwatz: got here too early, I think, life's a little bland, you?*
>*Me: it's ok here, lonely.*
>*Kwatz: miss you, you should've called earlier.*

That line always got me. Something familiar about it, or an attempt at familiarity. Did Kwatz think we had met before? Carl agreed that it didn't seem like an error in speech, we had too many iterations before to flush those out. Also, 'too early' and 'life's bland' stuck with me. We started to think this wasn't just shoegazing apathy. Although, that is my favorite way to flirt!

I started to think Kwatz meant that life, like organic life, was bland, as in not that complex where they had moved to. Moved too early. That was it, maybe they were colonizers, or observers of life. Able to sit on the wings for millions of years as life evolved upwards. Maybe that's why they assumed I would be busy having fun on Earth, everything teeming with life. Oh shit, that's when it hit me. Kwatz didn't know we were the indigenous race here on Earth! They think we're like them. Colonizers, or tourists.

>*Me: should I have? would you come?*
>*Kwatz: what?*
>*Me: nevermind, life's getting more interesting, wish you were here for the dinosaurs.*
>*Kwatz: wait, what?*

I was losing them, swinging wildly, not taking my own advice for prudence. But it seemed too late to back pedal. I had to go for it, as the hoard of project leads, bright minds, and overly thirsty bureaucrats hovered over my every keystroke. I tried to reclaim my status as the attractive popular girl.

>*Me: so... can I ask?*
>*Kwatz: go on.*
>*Me: why me? ;)*
>*Kwatz: why us, you mean ;)*
>*Me: haha*
>*Kwatz: billions of years is too long.*
>*Me: I understand* [*I didn't]
>*Kwatz: we should've never... diverged.*
>*Me: Split?*
>*Kwatz: yeah, too many splits, too many us. too many planets.*
>*Me: lonely.*
>*Kwatz: 'xactly.*
>*Me: come here, humans are fun. we can play.*
>*Kwatz: what are humans? You mean planet?*

Dammit, this wasn't going well. Did Kwatz really not know what a human was, after all this practice? Carl and I were getting worried that we couldn't maintain this ruse for much longer. Carl was trying to give me helpful advice. Maybe humans were just too small to think about for Kwatz. Maybe they only conceive of planets as collective, humans as insignificant as germs to them? Maybe Kwatz had been splitting and seeding the galaxy, just biding their time for other life to evolve into something else. Something more interesting to Kwatz. Or maybe, Kwatz just wanted their friend to finish consuming our world and return home. Before I could ponder my next approach, Kwatz struck first.

>*Kwatz: are you planet, or are you us?*
>*Me: ???*
>*Kwatz: tell me.*
>*Me: I'm not sure how to answer.*
>*Kwatz: are you Kwatz or are you other?*
>*Me: We are other. We are planet. We are human.*
>*Kwatz: ...*
>*Me: Please though. We want to learn. We want to know you. We want*
  to not be lonely too!
>*Kwatz: you are not like us.*
>*Me: I know but...*
>*Kwatz: c u later.*

The transmission ended. The signal went blank. A kill program swept our programs like a virus and shut down everything. And I mean everything. All records lost, except what we could remember and transcribe later. That was 25 years ago. And we haven't heard a single peep from any corner of the universe since.

***

Sorry, another sip of water. Do you have a tissue? Ha, no I'm OK, sorry phones going nuts in my purse, probably my nephew, he's in town, I said that right? Maybe we can take a break? Wait no, I'm ready to wrap for

134

the day. I am sorry, I didn't think this would get so emotional. Do you have one last question for me?

OK, that's two questions. So what do I think happened? And will we ever hear from them again? Hmm. I don't know. Maybe they're just a really private closed off species. Maybe they felt foolish for telling us too much. Maybe they found their other friend and they're laughing about the whole thing. Or, maybe that friend is already here, dormant, biding their time to take over. And will we ever hear from them again? Oh, I suppose that's sort of the same question. And I think I already answered it. But I'll say this, maybe the real answer is out there, if we listen for the sound of one hand clapping.

Prelude to the Silverwater Tavern, *a weird western*

"Silverwater would welcome you, but you've been here all along"

The Mojave desert sun was getting low and cool above this dusty, relic town of Silverwater. A radio broadcast from a distant rusted tower, on top of some rundown mechanics garage, bounces around the surrounding canyons called the Hollowlands, seeking its audience.

'Alright alright, fellow freaks, geeks and ghouls of the Hollowlands. You've been listening to Disco Pete's four o'clock magic hour, I'm Disco Pete, your guide through this netherworld of madness. It's a balmy but breezy 95 degree Thursday in the thirsty desert. You were just listening to a double dose of Radiohead for any of you paranoid androids and subterranean aliens. You also heard from Sioux on the Banshees, The Pixies, Duran Duran, & Bowie, all kicked off with 'White Rabbit' by Jefferson Airplane. Mixed in, a splash of cool from Miles Davis by special request. Some songs out of time for our man out of time - hope that helps the hangover, brother. Later tonight, our old timey radio, midnight marathon - adventures of time and space with special episodes of Dimension X... X... X! Weather, news and traffic at the six. But first up, some delicious beats for those cool and primitive drinks of water over at the saloon. Let's get strange out there tonight, you cowboys and aliens. This is Disco Pete for Hollowland's own Silverwater Radio, 91.9! Here's The Cramps with 'Primitive.''

***

Those low fidelity radio waves echoed along empty desert, through canyon walls and across open plains, searching for any signs of life in the lifeless terrain. And they always found the warmest welcome from a big wooden vacuum tube radio inside the only vintage hotel at the abandoned crossroads of town. The incongruously brilliant two story inn hung her sign above double batwing doors, reading simply: 'Silverwater Tavern.' The radio song hummed nicely inside an immaculate room of waxed floors, polished brass, and a glossy oaked wraparound bar at its center. The radio sat on the top of a beat up, hot pink jukebox, with tangled wires running all across shelved walls to worn down speakers. There was plenty of kitsch scattered about, from old vinyls, horse saddles, and polaroid cameras, to Tesla coils and other strange Davinci-like contraptions. None more out of place, amidst the carved crown molding and crystal chandelier, than the life-sized automaton man dressed as a blackjack dealer sitting behind a card table and plugged into the wall.

Behind the bar, underneath a tower of liquor bottles, tapped the boot of the tavern's dedicated caretaker, the beautiful barkeep who called herself Lyla. Lyla was pretty the way a rattlesnake is charming. Left arm fully sleeved in swirling tattoos, and the right stenciled with clean lines. She had long raven hair, often braided on both sides down to her waist. Today she had it tied up with a red banana, messy in her 'all business' bun. Lyla carried a rare sense of calm, comfortable in her skin, even in this eerie 'land of the lost' town. She spun her wardrobe across every era from 90's grunge to peace-child hippy, and even an occasional nod to her Comanche blood. Today she was in 80's metal, complete with sleeveless denim jacket, washed out Metallica tank, heavy on the eyeliner, and black studded wrist cuffs. She was perched in the back two legs of a barstool, thumbing her dimestore copy of "The Myth of Sisyphus" by Albert Camus, one eye on the clock, and her hard leather boots crossed on the bar with a sharp point that promised to tear a new asshole for any patron that disrespected her barroom rules.

The clock across the mantle, which was usually spinning out of control, had settled to a steady state and, as DIsco Pete had promised, was just past the witching hour of five o'clock. The low shift was waning to the wave of thirsty denizens, her regulars, already arriving at the side tables. A few sun-stroked cowboys in the front window table were playing slow poker hands like zombies. And there was Barnacle Bill, typically, posted on a stool by the service station, always too close, always in the way, always needing to be nudged aside like an arthritic old retriever sleeping too close to the fireplace. Lyla suspected old Bill was probably sleeping right now, upright and frozen stiff like a taxidermied man, although it was hard to say with his cloudy, dead, cataracted eyes.

Barnacle Bill claimed he had been a pirate, and a pretty successful one, before he decided to follow the boom of the Gold Rush up in San Francisco as a land-lubbing prospector. Layered in tattered vests, gold chains, a long 'always damp' trench coat (why was it always damp, he never went anywhere?), and a hat with an unturned front brim - his outfit certainly told the two tales of his life. The only time he really came alive was when peppered to tell a story from his days on the high seas or, better still, tales of stranger things mining across the mercury poisoned desert surrounding Silverwater.

The overhead lights began to flicker a bit, and like someone dropped their end of a piano up on the second floor, the chandelier rattled a large dust cloud into the air. Job was here. Lyla showed the tiniest corner of a smile. She grabbed the jukebox remote and switched it over from the radio, turning up the volume a little on the overhead speakers. Time to build some nightlife momentum with the hard drums of 'Goin Out West' by Tom Waits. And although she'd never admit it, it was for Job. And just as she turned back around, there he was, Job Branigan, private investigator.

Job conjured himself onto his usual bar stool, dressed in his well worn, well slept in, light gray suit. And it wasn't just his wrinkled suit that was on a grayscale. He seemed to follow the shadows like they were part of his wardrobe. And unless in direct sunlight, he seemed to emanate the hue of a silver era movie star. 'Anyone call for a detective?' Job knocked on the bar to announce his arrival, giving a courteous nod over to old Barney. Lyla grabbed a polished lowball glass and started a long pour of Jamesons neat. She pushed the glass in front of him with one hand, and used her other to present a neatly folded white bar mop. Job eyed the rag and sighed, 'Oh come on now, do I really have to wear a diaper?' Lyla just tilted her head, 'you know the rules, you old ghost.'

'Ghost? Please. I self-identify as a poltergeist.' Job put the towel neatly folded onto his stool and sat back down on it. 'But let's face it, I got too much Irish Jew stuffed in me to be anything else.' He gave his usual 'here's mud in your eye' toast and took a large swig of his whiskey. For a flash of a moment, his face pulsed with color, rosy and flush, before turning gray again. The whiskey drained its glossy path down his transparent throat, before drizzling down through him onto the absorbing towel below. 'Ah, that's life coming back, thanks, promise I'll try to hold onto the next one.'

'Rough night, Job? Quite the bender you're on lately,' Lyla mentioned the racquet he was making all night in the upstairs inn, harassing her guests no doubt, breaking more shit than usual. 'Any idea how long this one's gonna last?' She warned while pouring two shots this time, joining him. Job just shrugged sheepishly. She wouldn't take his money, only suggested he spend some time upstairs sweeping up the likely piles of shattered vases, glass, mirrors… frightened egos; all the usual aftermath from his fits. She turned and hollered back, 'And leave my damn guests alone when you're like that, you know, I always get a heavy ear-full from the big man.'

Job nodded more sincerely. 'Lookit I'm sorry, you said yourself they're all getting a little too comfortable here, and nobody knows what's waiting out there for them, not even us. What's the harm in me showing them a few scares, be good for them to confront some real terror.'

'Bumps in the night aren't the scariest things around this damned place'. Lyla corrected him. Job perked up at the mention of 'bumping in the night' and tried to make a lewd suggestion before Lyla stopped him. 'Pump those breaks, gumshoe, you're only on your second drink.'

Job took his time-out, grateful to catch his breath, still nursing his hangover, and rubbing his buried forehead on his folded arms. Cocking his head to the door, he noticed those three wranglers playing poker, slow like they were trying to fade into the background. Were they coming from cosplay at a dude ranch? Or were they actually cowboys? Then he muttered a bit confusedly, 'Don't I know those guys?' Job definitely remembered this sinister trio, he wasn't sure how, but thinks they were wearing black Italian suits. And maybe, gang tattoos, Russian mafia maybe? His memory seemed to be phasing in and out, even more than his body lately. And it would be hard to forget the big fellow, he was nearly seven feet tall, like some brown clay golem bursting through all that denim. Job swore he'd tangled with him before, was it last night, or last month? Lyla would never allow that in her bar. Must've been back on a case, something about Chinatown, a case he was working... or is working. God, his head was too fried for this, so he turned back to his whiskey and asked for a lager back.

'How's your case going, Job? What was it this time, some femme fatale, suspicious albi, a double blind?' Lyla was trying to help take his mind off the old cowhands. And it worked, Job put his elbows back on the bar and rubbed his temples, 'yeah, something like that, but I'm off duty, I think. Let me just solve the case of the missing Irish,' He rocked his eyes towards his empty lowball. 'Now, that case I can solve for you,' Lyla long poured another whiskey.

Before Job could touch his glass, he was shoved from someone passing, then knocked again by two others pressing up to the bar. Before he knew it, the bar was completely full, implausibly full! Shoulder to shoulder full of people out of nowhere. Job spun around in disbelief to see a hundred people? Two hundred? No, it couldn't be a thousand, not in this small bar. And all wearing the same torn jeans and yellow T-shirt. Was it the same person, he couldn't tell, his eyes darted around to get a better look, all he saw was blurry faces all in blurry yellow shirts. And they were everywhere. Yellow shirts at the jukebox, yellow shirts crowded around small tables, yellow shirts walking on the ceiling, sitting on the shelves, tossing themselves in the air, intruding behind the bar, pouring themselves drinks, And wait, was that, yes, one of the blurry face men was even shaking a tiny version of himself like a martini. Lyla was busy dispersing the mob with a sharp flicked towel.

'Is it just me or did this place get impossibly busy. There must be a million people here,' Job said in disbelief. Lyla sighed and corrected Job, it wasn't a million people, but an infinite amount of the same person. She had explained this to Job before but could tell he was still pretty hazy in the early twilight. And then it hit him, 'Ah ha. Particle-man just arrived!' Job remembered now, Particle-was a nice guy for someone caught between the quantum realm and this one. Had sort of crunchy 70's Caltech post-grad style, complete with birkenstocks and mad scientist hair, pinned down by a silly headband and silver bobbles. Usually a good drinking buddy, despite his horrendous physics puns, he was the embodiment of 'spooky action at a distance', as Einstein had said about all the bizarre things that happened at a quantum scale. And Job admired anyone with a craft for spookiness.

Lyla and Job happened to know that the only good trick to get rid of the crowd, the infinite probabilities of Particle-man, was to focus hard on just one of 'him'. So they both turned their attention to Job's left until the multitude of probability waves collapsed into one singularly observable man, sitting relieved on one single bar stool.

'Phew, that's better, the cat done died! Thank you for that, friends of Schrodenger.' The new patron sat upright and smoothed down his yellow tee that read, 'This shirt is blue… if you can run fast enough.'

'Our pleasure, how's everything shaking in the subatomic, Heisenberg?' Lyla tried to interrupt, warning Job that wasn't his name and not to encourage him.

'My love, I'm hurt, of course that's my name!' Particle-man mimicked a dagger to his heart, as he thumbed through the bar menu. 'In fact, that reminds me... where's your list of tequilas, oh my lord, look at all those. Would you pick one for me? I'm feeling a bit... UNCERTAIN.'

Lyla rolled her eyes, taking the menu away, reminding him last time he kept insisting his name was Planck, or was it Feynman. Particle-man pulled the menu back, and thumbed straight to the back, 'Well that's very true too! Reminds me I need help picking a dessert? I'm always divided by TWO PIs!' At that, he whipped around to Barnacle Bill, looking very pleased with himself. 'You get that one, Bill? Two Pi's... Planck's length? Divided by the... Jesus, read a math book, people.'

Lyla poured some clear Mezcal for the Particle-man. 'Rocks?' he suggested, a bit unsure. She raised an eyebrow, but he pressed on, 'I know, I probably shouldn't. You know I like to roll dice with the universe though.' And no sooner did she put ice in his glass, did the cubes start shaking violently into a buzzy vibration, just before hitting a crescendoed 'Pop!' and disappearing from the drink entirely. Lyla, slow and deliberate, moved his frozen disappointed hand two feet to the left, where an echoed 'pop' followed, and three ice cubes fell from the sky, plunking down right back into his glass. Grateful, Particle-man brought the glass delicately to his lips, but not before the whole glass this time started vibrating even more aggressively. It too disappeared from existence with a lip smacking 'pop!', echoing again, from the ceiling behind him, and dropping to a shattered mess across the clean floorboards. 'Sorry. Dammit.' Particle-man sighed, defeated.

Lyla leaned to Job, 'His drinks on you, by the way, for teeing up those jokes. I'll go grab a mop.' She disappeared after warning Job and Bill to keep one eye on this Schroeder's box so he didn't burst back into an infinite number of himself and the infinite amount of muddy feet that she'd have to mop. Heisenberg-Planck-Feynman (or whomever) perked back up, 'Hey, that's an interesting problem to solve, by the way. You can clean and mop up an infinite number of people's footprints... that's easy, you could do it in under a minute. Think about it...'

Job leaned in amused with the riddle. 'Let's see, I think I know this one. Well, I supposed I would spend 30 seconds mopping up after the first person's muddy tracks. Then I'd spend half that time, say 15 seconds on the second mess. Then half that time again for the next, and half again.

'Bingo!' Bill alarmingly yelled out from his coma in the corner. 'And on and on until you're spending fractions of seconds on each task, infinitely dividing in half, getting closer and closer, but never quite reaching one minute. But the question really would be, how do you ever get back to the bar if you're stuck mopping up infinity?'

Particle-man applauded silently, impressed, and took the invitation to go chat up Old Bill. So he rippled into eighteen shadows of himself, past and future, all walking around Job, before settling his trails into one seat again next to Bill. 'Now listen here, Barney, you've been a pirate right? Do you know what pirate's are supposed to do when they want to cut a physicist's joke short? No? You make me walk the Planck!'

Barnacle seemed unphased as he scrambled for the story he wanted to tell, 'Have I ever told you all about some meteor, that wasn't a meteor, done fell out the sky and turned into a clockwork man? Wait that ain't right.' Old Barney stammered on trying to start over.

Job took this opportunity to swing around to face Lyla in her busy work, deciding to try a different tact with his sweet talking. 'Hi, c'mere, Water Lily,' switched on his quieter charm, hooking his pinky with hers, leading her back in front of him. 'Listen, I'm sorry about all the broken shit upstairs, I guess I was hoping you'd come to punish me like the last time.'

He managed to elicit an eye roll, then a small blush in her cheeks. He leaned closer, and reminded her they could break a lot of things together if only she'd let him come haunting her room again.

Lyla finished her mopping and appeared back behind the bar, warming up some saki for a sullen woman seated at a dark corner table. 'Well, I have no idea what you're talking about, I work all night, so I couldn't have possibly ever spent the night with you.' Job reminded her she's always had a talent for being two places at once but she sparred back, 'Even if that were true, it would only have been a one time thing.' She waved her finger, walking away and smirking a little. Job knew enough to just pause and wait as she broke the silence with, 'maybe tonight.'

Job let her get back to her duties and announced, 'Sounds like the Doc just got here. And I'd lay a bet she's brought you some business.' Lyla asked how he could tell, after dropping the saki off to the quiet hooded woman. 'Please. I'm a detective, didn't you hear those shoddy bus tires squeal around the bend outside?' Then Job was reminded he better move to a darker corner, not wanting to scare off any of the new customers too quickly.

Just then the double doors burst open with the energy of eight, hooting and hollering, Ivy League college boys. 'SHOTS SHOTS SHOTS!' Luckily for them, they seemed to be chaperoned by one Doctor Maui Jean, the 'Doc'. A strange name considering she wasn't from Maui, but an entirely different ocean's island, Haiti to be exact. But she did wear a lot of Hawaiian shirts and smoked a lot of Pineapple Express. She had been a real doctor though, claiming she studied at Cambridge, but her practices leaned more now towards homeopathic stuff, like voodoo and other black magic. Regardless, having a witch-doctor slash drug dealer slash tour guide around came in handy more than one might expect.

The spoiled young sons of the upper elite made themselves at home, smacking on the jukebox, rearranging stools, and finger-gun pointing towards the weird cowboys in the corner. They were pretty typical hormonal, look-at-me, posturing college kids with hard-ons and popped collars. Meanwhile Doc blew past them, shaved head and flashy Elvis sunglasses, making her usual rounds and mail drops. She dropped a few packages wrapped in brown butcher's paper around to the tables, some cigarette cartons for Job, and then a special tight wrapped bag across the bar.

'What the hell is this?' Lyla asked while lining up a spread of the cheapest shots of gin on the rail. Maui Jean explained it was a peace offering, something green and stinky to keep her happy. 'That's not what I mean, who the hell have you brought me here?' Lyla had her hand on her hip.

Today, she seemed to have affected some caricatured Jamaican accent, either for her customers comfort or for her own amusement. 'Fresh meat, Queen Lyds! I picked 'em up side a the road wit' der broke down ass rental, on da way sum Spring Break road trip or sum ting. Promised I'd show 'em cosmic t'ings that would blow their damn minds out dis way! Course they're confused to 'ell on why dis town aint on no damn map. I said dis all part of da forbidden charm dat money can't buy. Course I took their money anyways."

The good Doctor Jean looked around suspiciously, before exchanging her islander's accent for her more familiar Essex one. She came in closer, 'Listen here now, love. Don't blow this for me, they're a good racquet a'ight? I've already made a monkey just smoking them up in the bus on the way here. And they tip like they're pissed off at their minted fathers, God love them American trust fund kids. I was going to take them out to the old UFO crash site tonight, skim a few more quid off 'em. Reckon they can stay here the night, maybe the Boss man wants them to stay longer, if you feel me?' The Doc flashed her bargainer's smile. 'I'll even waive my finders fee... for favors.'

'Let me make a call, but I don't like it. And I don't think the Boss will want them.' Lyla hopped on an old black wall mounted telephone and rang upstairs. 'And how the hell they get here anyways, the steam train?'

'Not unless that broke down train was pushing a Delorean.' Doc cueing Particle-man to add, 'Great Scott!' She then reminded Lyla it's her job to be out there scavenging the desert. And these clueless fools were just out there side of the highway, frozen in time, God knows how long, not knowing the world had moved on. Probably felt like minutes for them, bless their damned hearts.

Lyla multitasked, pulling eight pints of pilsner on reflex, as she muttered in a low whisper on the phone. The new horde did their shots, and dutifully paraded their pints around the place like tigers pacing around a cage. One of them took a seat next to Job but lost interest quickly when he started reciting The Ancient Mariner, playing the part of a real piss soaked drunkard. Particle-man was a bit nicer, keeping his composure best he could and enjoying some new company. When someone asked if they ever got live music, he mentioned that he can play *anything with strings but he was out of practice*. It was a 'string theory' joke that no one got, partly because it was too clever, but mostly because it was terrible.

One kid with ripped sleeves got the jukebox successfully clicked over to New Order's 'Blue Monday', and threw his fists in the air triumphantly. 'Gnarly! Bite me, turds, this tunes rad!' A few of them were poking around the set of stairs that led to the Inn's main hall. But Lyla shouted them back, saying it was closed, as she was wrapping up her call. They turned their attention instead to the blackjack booth with the odd little automaton dealer, and started pumping their bills into the flashing black box. Barnacle Bill, not doing a great job of looking normal - or really anything other than a taxidermist's stuffed attempt at a zombified gold miner - shouted over to them. 'Hey, have I ever told you about the silver city in the clouds up overhead? How one of their own silver metal men fell right off the edge?'

They all ignored him as the cocky alpha of the troop broke off to go harass the quiet saki drinking lady, shrouded in the shadows of her own hoodie. He tried flirting and traced his finger across her bare arms, which were marked wrist to shoulder with an impossible amount of tiny criss-crossed scars. The razor thin lines almost resembled an elaborate tattoo design, and he used it as his opening, asking playfully if she liked to play with knives. Lyla drew his attention back over with a fresh round of gin shots, like a pro, and probably saved him getting his arms chopped off.

'Here, come harass me instead, handsome,' as she hung up the phone and made a louder announcement. "Good news, bad news gentlemen, we're closing down in an hour for renovations, you can order as much as you can drink in that time, and this rounds on me.' They echoed back in applause, while Lyla shot her told-you-so glance at the Doc, who didn't seem to care too much. The good Doctor Jean was two steps ahead, already starting to stock up her bus's beer coolers. She figured she could skim a few more bucks off these lads one way or another. Some of them were shouting already to push through to Vegas, but she'd maybe talk them into the full 'Area 51' experience. Even if they didn't want to pay for it, it would be worth the look on their faces when they see what's crawling around out there.

The boys were getting well riled up, dividing their oglings between the mysterious girl in the corner and Lyla behind the bar, catcalling her everytime she reached up for a bottle and giving them a good view of her tight midriff. 'I would be a lot more careful sassing any ladies in this place,' warned Lyla. The college boys scanned around the bar with their devil-may-care look smirks. But Lyla wasn't talking about the other bar patrons. Sure they could get whipped up into a tussle, maybe cause a little trouble and a few black eyes. But she explained that the only real bouncer around here was the dealer in the corner, pointing to the cobwebbed metal robot, lifelessly turning over blackjack cards for two of the boys, who were suddenly aware of the group's attention.

'Is that right? Stand aside fellas,' said the cocky frat president, rolling up his sleeves, as he swaggered over to get eyeball to eyeball with this robot dealer in a green visor. He knocked on his head looking for anything menacing. And the robot's eyes answered with tiny red flashes, sputtering and strobing with the slow turning sounds of an awakening movie projector. 'This old gadget doesn't look like much to me.'

'No, she's right,' chimed Job from the cheap seats, always happy to let a good horror story do his dirty work, leaving him to mind the business in front of him. 'That there is Wiretop Wyatt, and he doesn't tolerate anything less than chivalry towards the ladies in this saloon.'

'Wiretop Wyatt! Right, oh, that's it, now I remember my story!' Jumped Barnacle Bill nearly jumped out of his stool, which was as startling as a stuffed cat pouncing onto your lap. 'Have I ever told you the story of Wiretop Wyatt? The robot who fell from the sky and laid waste to an entire town of raiders and rustlers.' Old Bill started walking around the bar touching each kid on the shoulder like a game of duck-duck-goose, as he told his ominous tale with his cold dead eye holding their attention. 'Oh he learned how to hate, for a robot. And he hated bullies worst of all. But just before he was called Wyatt, the robot with a tangled mess of wires springing from his head like an electrician's worst nightmare, before all that, he was simply a silver streak across the sky. A silver streak like a falling satellite, burning up hot in the desert sky, this robotic man crash landed onto soft and hostile alien dunes, unfamiliar with the ways of the Wild West. At least, at the start.'

Lyla kept the shot glasses full as the boys gathered, mesmerized by the somber tale of strange justice. Particle-man and Job closed their eyes, imagining that they were hearing it for the first time. Even the kids playing blackjack, abandoned his post to join the drum circle. Everyone was so gripped with Barnacle Bill's tale, no one seemed to notice that the supposed leader of this pack was not listening at all, left staring at the arcade contraption of a man. Frozen and squatting, his eyes transfixed to the glowing red eyes of that metalman dealer, previously lifeless, now appearing to stare right back. The kid was hypnotized by piercing strobe lights, speeding up like a film reel about to tell a different story. A story the boy already knew, the one that he tried so hard to forget, and resided deeply buried and festering in his darkest dreams.

Hypnotized, still frozen, he saw in those robot eyes his own disturbing memories. A fraternity house party. An orgy of pills, beer kegs, and sorority girls. The hooked attraction of an innocent girl, spilled drinks, stumbling and dizzy. Her foggy disappearance to an upstairs bedroom, and his pursuit to find her. So playful at first. Hide-and-seek, followed by hard-to-get. Her resistance. His greedy hands. Her scratch on his face. His violent grip. And then… silence. Ghastly silence.

'NO!' The boy snapped himself from the trance, interrupting the yarn Bill was spinning to the rest. Everyone spun around shocked to see him out of breath and trembling. The eyes of the metalman had gone dim, and lifeless. The boy, now feeling so uncorked by the shame of his past, was hit with a tidal wave of shame, the contempt of every woman, every person, he had mistreated his entire life. And his latent guilt now turned itself into a raw and gripping terror. The terror of a wounded animal now acutely aware that the wolves were coming, stalking him, bloodthirsty for the kill.

So he jumped up in his panic, dropped a fifty dollar bill on the counter and rounded everyone up. 'Sorry fellows, no time for this story, we got to go.' He feigned a confident rally cry assuring his comrades the fun would continue on the road. Off to Joshua Tree, as intended, maybe that UFO crash site their guide has been promising, then Vegas. The group was a little confused with the abruptness of it all, but reluctantly fell in line as they pushed off their stools, taking their final swigs of beer, and following their trembling tribe leader to the bus.

Barnacle only paused his story long enough to watch them go and shake his head in pity. 'I bet those poor fellas wouldn't be in such a fuss to leave if they knew there's no place to go outside the Hollowlands. And that they can never go back home.' Job returned to his empty stool, and the rest of them leaned in to hear the rest of the tale, as Lyla switched the jukebox back over to the old wooden box radio.

***

Good evening, my strange bedfellows, canyon raiders, legs of jello, lullabied by undead bellows. The sun's stalling low at this seven o'clock hour but the shadows are still getting longer, in case you haven't made haven't yet made camp safely from the waking desert canyon's vampires. And for all those early rising harpies, happy hunting tonight. You've been listening to Disco Pete's sunset drive time hour, I'm Disco Pete, your guide through this existential voyage through the hollowlands, Silverwater radio, 91.9. You've heard music by the Cramps, Led Zeppelin, and Depeche Mode, as well as a little ditty by our tavern's own Barnacle Bill - in case you're catching on by now, things work real weird around these parts. We're all one consciousness experiencing our own false sense of individuality through non-linear, subjective expressions after all. We'll resume that tale about our revenging robot crash landing here from his low orbit after the hour. Traffic, weather and UFO high alerts, just after a few words from our sponsor, Winston Cigarettes. Mmm, tastes good like a cigarette should.

The Hermit and the Bear, *a wilderness fable*

Once upon a time, there lived an old hermit in the wilderness of a deep forest who was tormented every night by a surly, burly old grizzly bear. Every evening, the bear would make her rounds to the man's small cabin on a sunny clearing from the grove. And every night, the man would lock himself in tightly, cowering through the lonely cold winter; the shadow of the bear always stalking him in the distance.

The bear would trounce the man's gardens through the night, so the hermit could no longer grow fresh food. The bear would chase away the birds, so that the hermit had no beautiful songs to greet him in the morning. The bear would howl like thunder through the day, until the hermit was convinced it was always too stormy to go outside. Night after night, the hermit lost sleep to his own imagined terror of hot misty breath coating his tiny single paned window. And he was plagued by the notion that the bear had summoned many others, prowling the surrounding dark forest.

So the hermit kept quiet and festered in his, once peaceful, now scuttled solitude. He would shake his head, hands grasping his ears, fearfully and defiant of sleep. The hermit would scream his curses out loud, while he ate canned beans and tried to remember the taste of blueberries. He would hum and drum quietly on his table, trying to remember the sound of music. Inevitably, he was always interrupted by the far off guttural bellow of his gnarly, grizzly bane.

For days and nights, the hermit would curse his tormentor and call out into the darkness the many names he had made for the bear. He would call him the demon, hell's abomination, the darkness, the deceiver, the destroyer... the man eater, the dream killer! And in those names, he imbued all of his problems, the excuses for his plagued mind. He would cry, "curse and spit upon you, demon from hell, my famine, my robber of sunshine, my prison warden!" And curses, he did spew, from his window and from his bed, spitting and shaking fists with rage against the darkness. Until eventually, the hermit knew no other pastime, forgetting his prayers and meditations, forgetting the hope of music and the sweetest in food, only latching on to his rage for this wicked forest demon.

Meanwhile, there stood the bear, alone at the ridge of her forest, head cocked to the side, curious and confused by the strange noises from that small cabin. The bear delighted in the many wonders of this sunny grove, and took delight in its treasures. There were birds to chase, there were wild blueberries to pick, the cabin had large posts for her to scratch her back. And inside that cabin, there was even a funny little man that liked to play peek-a-boo from the curtains. It was a fun game that soothed her disquietude. For the bear had grown lonely in this deep dark forest. And when the thunder came cracking, she took shelter in the canopy, weeping loud and terrified at the angry heavens. The only thing that gave her comfort was hearing the shouting war cries of the funny little man, defiant of the thunder, and answering her whimpers with a call to courage. More and more, the grizzly bear felt at peace, coming around every night, dancing and shouting as the man did, nestled under his slumbering window, feeling safe.

One particularly vicious and stormy night, the hermit could hear no more. He spent so much of his fury and despair, shaking fists as his unknown tormentors, this bear and her company of beasts, all twelve feet tall and bloodthirsty. As the howls of the unknowns beat against his cabin window, he decided there and then to confront this beast, to see her with two eyes and to name his fear. Afterall, if it was only one bear, she should only have one name. And that by giving one fear, one worry, one bear, so many names, the man was suffering the onslaught of an army of bears inside his head.

So the hermit swung open his cabin door, and leaped faithfully into the mud to confront his devil. The hermit paused in that moment, scanning the treeline for Chimera herself. But all he saw, huddled low, was one lonely bear, shivering scared in the rain, and trembling with a longing look. The hermit, still wary, beat his fists across his chest and bellowed a warcry of defiance to the sky. And in that moment, he saw something unexpected. A tiny smile swept across the bear's face, one of admiration and reassurance. The bear beamed with respect and loyalty for the man who showed her how to find her courage.

Not forgetting his promise to give the bear a name, the hermit thought of the only word he felt he had lost, one that needed to be spoken more, for both him and the bear. He knelt and he whispered the bear's new name: Valor. And from that night forward, amidst all the demon's of his mind, he called out for Valor. Every night, and amidst every wrap against his window, a change began to take hold. His relationship with the many shadows lurking along the dark treeline, the many wicked usurpers of the winter, became just one named and familiar beast. One lonely bear, named Valor.

Spring arrived to warm the hermit's days, and he abandoned a winter stove for an open fire outdoors each night. He enjoyed the labors of cooking slowly, while calling softly to his new shy neighbor. Valor liked her new name, holding her head higher, as she spent less time hiding away, and more time rolling around the fresh grass by the warmth of the man's fire. As spring stretched to summer, the man began sharing his meat from the fire, often feeding Valor by the hand. And before long Valor and the hermit became friends.

So after a long dark winter, the revival of spring, and the dawn of the summer sun, an old hermit and a lonely bear found something they didn't even know they were looking for. Peace in each other's company. A shared valor against the confusion of so many imagined fears, valor against shapeless worries, valor for one's unnamed unknowns. The hermit gained this golden apple of wisdom as cure for his solitude, and felt fortunate enough, as wise men do, to share it with his new friend.

"My best friend, Valor", he whispered, "Your fears are there to be named, your beasts take shape as such to be tamed, and happiness is our right to proudly reclaim."

Book II: Risings & Ramblings, *the literary fiction*

A Relegated Ship, Run Aground, *a*
postmodern Dublin city tale

Part One: A Relegated Ship, Run Aground & Derelict

She was an old merchant ship, the oldest remaining in Ireland, moored to rest along the banks of the Grand Canal. She was named the Naomh Éanna (Neev Ay-na). Completed in Dublin's Liffey Dockyard in 1958, sailing in her prime as an Aran Islands ferry, she laid now in her graving dock back in Dublin, overdue for demolition since 1989. Some local petitioning had campaigned to list her as a heritage vessel with little success. Throughout the quibbles and competing ideas on restoring her purpose, ranging from river ferry to museum to boutique hotel, she waited patiently and hopefully leaning crooked in a muddy embankment. She was enclosed by barbed wire and graffitied walls on a restricted lot of wild grass. Her metal rails were rusted, her bones were frail. This lonely derelict now wears a fresh badge of spray paint, pleading simply, 'Don't Scrap Me.'

Discarded and struggling to remain relevant. You know a thing or two about the feeling, and find comfort gazing upon this old relic. Since the last pandemic, life has felt a bit stalled. Dublin has always been a symbol of risings and renewals in your heart. Moving here just before the centennial of the 'Easter Rising' for Irish independence, you immediately felt the spirit of rebellion and resilience among the native born Irish. Maybe you had missed 'The Troubles,' and three decades in conflict, but you felt their shadows in every pubside chat. Maybe you arrived too late to see the rise and fall of a booming 'Celtic Tiger', but you felt intrinsically linked to Dublin's new rising, rebuilding a new hope for endless prosperity.

***

He was a houseless tattered man, the most tenured local denizen to live off the sidewalks near the Grand Canal. He was named Adam, like the first man, or so you've been told by local store clerks who know him best from his daily routines. His territory for scavenging loops along the South Wall, Pearse Street and Ringsend, ending in the protected basin where the Naomh Éanna also sulked each evening. And no one shared Naomh's discarded abandonment better than this broken man, the rough sleeper who camps under her chipped feet and rusted bones, in the same walled off land owned by the same national asset manager who took over all the disenfranchised lands of the prior housing crisis. Adam's whole demeanor, from his bulldog walk, mud caked sweatpants and cut up hands, to his long greasy hair and twitchy outbursts, all shout, "Please don't snub me."

Discarded and struggling to remain relevant. You know a thing or two about the feeling. You had been an observer of Adam's from afar for over ten years now, fascinated with his lifestyle, his routines, his survival instinct. Adam was known well in this neighborhood, a mascot of sorts, regarded with small tokens of kindness by some and treated indifferently by many. He cut a frightening path to many families in the neighborhood, who veered away when they saw him approaching or digging through the rubbish bins. He wasn't a meth addict, or a drunk, or a beggar, or a criminal. As the local shop owners have told you, he doesn't speak English well, but he shows respect and appreciation for his surroundings, always paying dutifully for his modest purchases when he has the coin. He is chemically off-kitler, maybe a little deranged, or just dialed into some other layer of reality the rest of us can't access. Everyday he walks the open town square with his stout gate, making his rounds, seemingly shaking out bad thoughts, muttering loudly and sometimes even laughing hysterically at the rich conversations in his head. Your life feels entangled with his. And anytime you catch yourself in your own head, lost in your seemingly important problems, there he appears, conjured up, a force of nature, like a mirror in everyone's face, reminding us of our fragility, nudging us towards a quiet gratitude. And you desperately wished to know him, to commune by coin or kindness, or just to help him feel less invisible.

***

You have been an outsider looking in, you've seen remnant fragments and fractures in a city that had grown up in a big old hurry. Your name didn't matter much, you're just another foreign national riding the wave of Dublin's new economy. But the name of your neighborhood is the Grand Canal, often referred to as the 'Silicon Docks' in deference to the pipeline of technology money that Ireland invited from Silicon Valley's tech firms. In your decade living here, you've seen many changes washing over this pale city divided by the River Liffey. And like that mighty river, the city flows both ways, changing often with the tides of the time.

Despite the bubble bursting after 2008, there was no slowing down the juggernauts of the tech companies like Google and Facebook, occupying this modernized neighborhood of Grand Canal Square. You were a part of this employment boom, welcoming diverse talent from near and far with open arms, but you've never really felt like the protagonist in this story, just an extra in the broader redemption arc of Dublin, just a splash of color in her narrative. You watch the rising tides with awe and wonder, nonetheless. Banks started dishing out cheap loans again, rebates, free money. Everyone propped themselves up on these precarious stilts of wealth, whilst proudly shaking their fists at history, crying defiantly 'this prosperity will endure for all of time! This time, this time it will last.'

Arriving in those resilient days, you found a city scarred and jaded, but licking its wounds in hopeful fashion. The famed Irish concrete and construction industry had been very busy gobbling up the old and discarded. New bridges and commercial highrises stood proudly, the moguls liberally scattered the hastily assembled hotels and condos, and everyone scrambled for their piece of the fast selling pie. You moved into one of those posh condos slapped together in a hurry, luxurious but a little slanted at the seams. A grand panoramic view across the Liffey, it was not hard to imagine your view as a historical storyboard. From left to right, you glance across the North Wall Quay, telling the tale of the harp shaped Samuel Beckett bridge, the large pint glass shaped Convention Centre. And off to the east, you see the stalled construction plans of Point Square; a planned mall, hotels and a concert arena. Punctuated deadcenter along the storyboard was a derelict tower that was commissioned to be the new headquarters for the Anglo Irish Bank, the institution that led to the last financial collapse.

This embodiment of a destitute district stood solitary, stripped bare and exposed to the elements. A phantom reminder of the past, telling her foreboding lesson on the impulse to overreach. Just like the Spire of Dublin, also erected in surging times, this old relic knew a thing about tempting fate with its notions of 'prosperity stretching to the heavens, unshakeable and endless.'

Part Two: Invisible Mobs & Monsters

By the centennial year of the 1916 Easter Rising, the spirit of Dublin started to sing again, a song of redemption. The bones of the economy and the investments in finance and tech were paying dividends. The commercial real estate engine started revving again, as these global tech giants kept printing a seemingly endless stream of money. Consequently, through the 2010's, the Dublin skyline was lush with construction cranes, splashing their nightlights across the dark rapid river. The last jigsaw piece of the old busted Celtic Tiger was now being reconciled, with the Central Bank of Ireland setting its sights to reboot construction on that stalled Anglo Irish project. You've enjoyed feeling part of this rebirth, peering across the river from your high rise flat. As the newly assembled construction crew speeds towards completion, you marvel at how the designers for a central bank would call for it to be finished in a glimmering gold. You begin to understand why the phoenix bird longs to burn herself to ashes, exchanging betrayed memories for endless new beginnings.

By the next decade's pandemic, you watch as the wheels come off the machine again, dozens of buildings finished but now unoccupied. Dublin followed the lead from Silicon Valley's chosen path to persevere, promising investors and the public continuous wealth throughout the lockdown. Pivoting to catch all the virtual workflow money bubbling up in the 'work from home' era. Then over-speculating on the trend and pivoting again with massive layoffs, the fashionable trend to appease shareholders. Only to rehire again quickly to justify those large empty corporate buildings, standing dormant and expectantly, as the companies test a big 'back to the office' push. Whether working from home or in office was proven definitively to be more productive, a city propped up on commercial real estate would be clamoring for this return. The tide comes in, the tide goes out, and on and on it goes.

Like a factory assembly line stalling hard and speeding back up, inevitably boxes fell off the conveyor belt, and people got left behind. You rode these shift changes yourself, riding high on an arena stage in a glass tower, then sitting low in a social welfare office squeezed between similarly displaced corporate professionals. You scanned around the room of job seekers, twenty-five people receiving aid in a group presentation, twenty-four of them middle-aged men like you with the same defeated look. They all seemed to be puzzling through the disbelief and betrayal from their respective industries, the ones still towering rich along the prosperous Dublin skyline. Sitting patiently through a compulsory, antiquated presentation about occupational skills, probably from the nineties, their eyes still shine a glint of gratitude for any offer of support. But underneath that, there's a frustration in feeling invisible and misunderstood in a city failing to keep up with the unemployment trends speeding along like a runaway train. Each diverse and forlorn face whispers it, struggling to remind the city of the boom party it had invited them to, 'you promised us a share, we're still here waiting, we still matter.'

***

When lockdown eased in the city, the sidewalks resumed the beating pulse of routine commuters. Facemasks started coming off, handshakes were accepted, people lingered outdoors and restaurant pre-bookings waned, leaving more room for spontaneity. None so grateful, strode Adam along the rejuvenated bustle of the Grand Canal Square. He's never relied heavily on the tech commuters for hand-outs, never seen panhandling with an open cup. In the worst of rainy days, he's seen rifling through the public square's bins just after the lunch crowd peaks. In sunnier days, he's seen receiving kindness from the locals and cafe workers, a store bought sandwich, a cup of ramen, a place to sit on the patio during off-peak hours. Relegated to a dark sidewalk corner table but treated with respect, reminded of his fortune to feel part of the neighborhood. This was how Adam recharged his dignity.

As the big tech towers drew a new affluent group of young professionals with disposable income, Adam also thrived, not only by handouts, but by the humanizing feeling of belonging to a community thriving. And you worry that during the times of lockdown he was more vulnerable than anyone to an abrupt cut-off of those simple reminders. During the restrictions, Adam had disappeared, with only the odd traces of his presence. A tattered sleeping bag twisted up in the wild grass behind that fenced off restricted lot. Small glimpses of his figure cutting a shadow far in the distance. But as life returned to the square, so did his spirited shadow begin to linger a bit longer in the day, resiliently climbing back into the sun.

It's during one of those high tide days, when things are going your way again and you find yourself at a new job. Skipping busily between your new office and a quick lunch break along the square, when you see Adam again. It was a sunny midday in the summer, and instead of his usual scurried routines, you are surprised to see him sleeping peacefully, the way a child sleeps, curled up on his side on a warm park bench. You take comfort in his vulnerability, knowing that everything in Adam's world is spinning reliably again. As the world begins to provide, there is time again to dream of tomorrow.

And as this calm washes over you, you notice a small construction crew taking their lunch break, snickering and taking pictures of Adam fast asleep. You keep walking, glancing behind to see them huddled around, prodding each other to take selfies, laughing and pointing at his soiled trousers. As Adam awakes from the bullying, you feel compelled to intervene, shouting out, and waving a finger of warning to the young mob, a reminder to show some respect. Afterall, who among us could pretend we were not vulnerable to a life like Adam's. The startled lads disperse quickly at your nudge, and Adam stands up to shuffle past you, barely perturbed, eyes averted and offering no sign of familiarity.

Weeks went by until you see Adam again, shifting his weight, standing outside the local market. This time you make sure to try harder, to stop and show that you were a friend, an ally. You say his name and again, like a skittish fox, he seemed more eager to retreat. But this time, he lifts his head a little higher and flashes you one tiny sparkle of recognition. He knows you, and he knows you know him.

He'll never say hello again, or reply when you call his name, but every day forward when you see him, you call out and fish for money from your pockets. Without turning, he pauses for you to catch up, accepts your coins, and continues proudly on. You forget why it was ever so important that he knows you, but you're glad that you now see each other, exchanging warmth and solidarity. In this moment, you had something in common, accepting the hand of a comrade, without shame, and happy to feel part of a tribe. You recall the faces of those twenty-five displaced professionals, and despite the obvious opportunity to blame the world for casting a cold eye, you resist, as you've never seen the look of blame in Adam's face. His armor shone bright and polished with a battle tested sense of dignity.

***

Despite the slow creeping revival of so many others, the Naoimh Éanna unexpectedly falls over, demanding attention from the local news and social feeds. The attempts to salvage her have been deemed a failure. The various campaigns waning, the ship had been pillaged and scuppered by vandals over the years, and the popular opinion turning their back on her hopeful spirit. Casting stones, and deeming her an eyesore, useless and inconvenient to our important lives and our newly gentrified square. The social mob lynched her with biting disregard, the pressure mounted, calling for her immediate removal by the Irish Ship and Barge Company.

You read about this from a cafe along the docklands, reflecting on the shame people like Adam must have to wrestle back, defying feelings of irrelevance, persevering through solitude, disregarding any inconvenience to others. After witnessing so many ebbs and flows, you realize you don't have to be homeless, or decommissioned, or disabled, or unemployed, to wrestle with these demons. There are no limits to who can fall vulnerable or disenfranchised. And there are no boundaries for the empathy they all deserve. Suffering is suffering, no matter your station. We do what we can to avoid chaos, to find purpose, and feel accepted. Depravity or despair, which comes first? Revival or perseverance, does one always follow the other? Ask Adam, ask the Naoimh, ask those twenty-five people sitting in a government office. The desire to feel significant, the urge to keep living, beats in each of them.

While the River Liffey begins filling high again, you follow the current back to office work with the masses, reminding yourself repeatedly to never take for granted the fragility of Dublin's mercurial tides. You make your way over to the sunken basin where that old merchant ship leans, moored to rest along the Grand Canal. You see all the summer kids in wetsuits, climbing the fence, jumping off from The Naoimh's bow into the water, and kicking around a twisted up, old sleeping bag. You can imagine the way The Naoimh carved through the gloriously rough waters of the Aran Island in her prime. You think of your own glorious high sailing adventures and ponder the many voyages ahead of you still.

You whisper to yourself and on behalf of all those who feel like you, your petition to the towers overhead; you plead with grace and humility. 'Please, please, don't scrap us yet.'

Tiny Dormant Treasures

meditations in my fathers garden

You walk the garden and you feel them buried beneath. There's an energy humming, a vibration of life, something sleeping, something wonderful, waiting in the dirt and the darkness. But waiting for what? The right conditions? The perfect season? Their best chance to be observed and admired by the best audience? You wonder what keeps such tiny treasures dormant and why they hide their beauty from the world.

Sometimes they are seeds, treasure boxes packed full of potential energy, just waiting to be activated. Like the precocious acorn, buried and forgotten by some hungry squirrel, winding up to become a mighty oak tree. Sometimes it's even creepier creatures, not so imbued with grace, but just as triumphant and mighty. Like the seven year cicadas, larva buried deep in the ground, cradled in darkness, surviving cold frozen winters, and connected by some soft rhythm, some universal alarm clock to say when it was time to emerge and burn their short bright life. Sometimes they're the little twigs and buds of a cherry tree or a dogwood. Dead sticks and branches all winter long, waiting patiently, sleeping deeply, and then bursting their bouquets and painting the treeline with such a majestic glow that all matter of bird, bee and beast must bow in worship.

As you dig for weeds, reposition your garden and begin to lay down mulch for the season ahead, you spot the poppies and almost mistake them for milkweed. You leave them be and realize they'll be 'popping', as they do, their burnt orange vanities by Memorial Day weekend, just in time to replace all the fading tulips in the garden bed. Out with the old, in with the new. And you can't help but pause and ponder the mysteries of the invisible, wondering what other little sleeping beauties are lying two feet below your knees... and why they're there.

These strange perennials of the garden and the cycles they've adapted seduce and fascinate you on this late spring day. Plants evolved in such a way to spend most of their time hibernating, living off last season's sunny reserves, one eye open waiting for the right conditions and then bursting to life for a few short weeks, maybe a month, screaming in hubris at anyone willing to gaze, "Look at me! Bow to my glory"! Then fading again and falling back to sleep.

It's the poppies, the elephant ears, the alliums, the montauk daisies, the hydrangea. All of them, nestled, cocooned into their bulbs, those tiny treasure boxes, waiting for their turn to burst and be seen. Tiny and dreaming of being something grander. You think then about all those little things inside you, buried just beneath the surface. Those tiny treasures of your personality, your capabilities, your unrealized potential, all wound up tightly like a ball of rubber bands, waiting to be stretched beyond containment, snapped out into the world. You think of the way you've waited so patiently for your next big job, your next big role, and a chance to express yourself differently as a professional, catching the attention from a busy world.

You think about the creative expression you yearn to foster, things smoldering inside, waiting to be engulfed with flame, like the many little stories, outlines and ideas you have laying dormant two feet under the surface in your head. Ideas waiting to become something more, dreams yearning to grow into words, words searching for the fertile grounds of other ears, other minds. And stories that can shine in ways that spread joy and inspire grace.

Creativity catches the eyegaze of one's soul, catches fire and beckons the attention of birds, bees and beasts. And you wonder again, why do all these things - bulbs, seeds, buds, larva... ideas, dreams, ambitions, desires - why do they sleep at all? And how do we ever know when it is time to stir them from that slumber, when will they come out to bloom?

Soon, you should hope. Soon and not for long. It's that fleeting notion that helps you slow the ticking clock of expectations. It's the fragility of expectant flowers that soothes you. It's the promise of a neatly wrapped present that delivers giddy joy in the tomorrow. And for now you dig reverently in the dirt, you pause, then breathe deeply and hold onto the promise of unseen treasures arriving in their own time.

A Frightful Fiend Doth Tread,

an essay on existential dread

I recall staring lost across the grassland abyss of the Serengeti. A seemingly infinite savannah stretching to curved horizons in all directions, like standing in the middle of a small moon, both deceived by the promise of endlessness and trapped by her curvature. I remember at this moment seeing nothing threatening, but feeling the stalking threat of probabilities.

Deep in the bush, that's all there are - possibilities. Infinite realities waiting to collapse into a realized one - just for me, the observer. This wilderness of east Africa wasn't intrinsically hostile or evil. But it was cold and dispassionate to those intruders wandering into its kingdom, confused by its void and pleading for its borders. But not me. In one small moment in time, I found myself walking out towards its flat open horizons like an astronaut stepping off his station into open space. In each step I took away from the vehicle that brought me onto this open plain was a feeling of separation from order and protection.

Today was supposed to be the day I deepened my retreat into this wild rite of passage through Africa. I had taken the day off from my volunteering assignment, mixing concrete for a school in the village of Endulen, Tanzania; deep in the Maasai territory of Ngoro Ngoro. I picked up with a few other friends and paid two locals to be our driver and guide for a safari expedition in the local church's old Toyota 4Runner. We were well off the map on this off-roading day trip to parts unknown of the Serengeti. The impossibly vast savannah wasn't a national park the way you would expect to see families out for the weekend, endurance hikers and camper vans clustered about. This was chaos in every direction, the land that time forgot. The sparsely dotted acacia trees did little to break up the landscape, instead reinforcing the endlessness like a fractal pattern that kept changing and getting further away the closer you looked. This was the surface of Mars, this was outer space, this was the middle of the Atlantic ocean - indifferent to my presence and cruel to my needs. This was Africa.

And there I was, wanting to get lost in it and scream into its wide open mouth. As I stood there at the edge of space, I had this overwhelming sense of loneliness and a shudder overtook me with a horrid dread for all the unknown fiends in every direction. They were not in sight but when you are dealing with the infinite you must assume every possibility is out there, lurking and waiting patiently. Wanting to feel this deep surrender into the wild, I took a few more paces away from the car, wondering when I would feel the untethering, like cutting the rope to my liferaft. I was treading water in the middle of the ocean, sharks swimming in the distance, right below me, or hundreds of miles away. Unaware of my presence or faintly picking up my scent, each pace I took across this tightrope of uncertainty, gave these monsters another spin at being aware of me. This land was entropy's playground.

Before long and to the distress of my group, the old Toyota that brought me here was only a small black dot in the distance. I began to dread that it could disappear out of existence entirely behind me, just as new objects could appear blinking from nothingness into my path. Every step felt a deeper descent to chaos, each minute spent wandering brought me deeper into darker possibilities. One step closer to a wild animal, one extra roulette spin to see what hyena will catch my scent, one small agitated air vibration hitting the ears of a leopard. I was perturbing waters that wished only to be impartial. You could even feel the tension in my guide as he turned over the engine, calling me back in. He was taking me to the edge of Chernobyl, fulfilling his duty for pay, but growing impatient for me to just take my damn selfies so we could make our desperate retreat.

Earlier in the day I had been invited to many other moments of horror but had politely declined. At one point, we were meant to find a spot for lunch so our guides spotted a good little oasis with some long shade and downed trees to sit on. The safety trick, they explained, was to drive a few laps aggressively around the trees first, revving engines and honking furiously, to flush out anything hiding out in the bushes. So we did that for a while with no sign of danger and set up our little tourist picnic. Shortly into my sandwich, the guides got a bit jittery and pointed out some leopard tracks circling around where I was sitting. Based on their freshness and some even fresher droppings, they probably weren't more than an hour old. I couldn't help glancing over my shoulder at the thick brush behind me, expecting that slow fisheye-lens dolly shot you'd sometimes see in a horror movie towards some cloaked and guttural panting. And yet, I felt nothing, took a bite of the rest of my sandwich and slowly packed back up.

Later in the day, another moment of danger came knocking. We had crossed paths with a ranger who was out tracking lions tagged with RFID collars and kindly offered to pull out his antennae equipment and point us in the right direction. We followed his truck for a while, to find two behemoths, male and female lounging out under a tree. It was my first time seeing big cats like this in the wild and the tears of joy abounded as I snapped photo after photo. All the excitement ended however when again the guides started to jostle uncomfortably, explaining as delicately as they could to us that that car battery had died. I sat patiently, marooned in a hot car in the middle of nowhere, watching one of the drivers bang away

177

on the engine with a hammer, while the lions started to circle. All I could think about was how great the photos were going to be. Again, an invitation for horror, unaccepted.

As an avid horror fan, I remember reading Stephen King's description of his defined levels of fear in writing. The first and probably the most shameless is the 'gross-out' level. That would be when I got to see these lions rip my guides from limb to limb in a bloody orgy of rage. Cinematic, but not very interesting to me. The second level is called 'horror', this is where you see the monster and are confronted with the looming danger, face to face. This was that moment of those lions pacing about. Scary, sure, but leaving very little to the imagination. Then there's the third level known as 'terror'. This is the monster in your closet, waiting, lurking, unseen. This was the leopards, or probable leopards, lurking with uncertainty in the bushes. They were there and not there, and none so terrifying or teeth so sharp as how they exist in your mind's eye. And still, I felt nothing.

And then finally, there was me at our last stop of the day, wandering far off from the car and staring against a sprawling plain of infinite possibilities. If I were to write to Stephen King, I would be proposing to him this moment as the prime case study of a 4th level of fear, the one I would name 'dread'. This was the monster under your bed times a million. This was the dread of decisions and indecisions leading to any collision course in your life. This was swimming in the open ocean and not knowing what hungry jaws, squid leg or drowning fatigue would rise up to snatch you first. This was living out a thousand deaths in each one of your days, wondering if today would be the day some car sideswipes you on your bicycle. Dread is the sheer invitation from chaos to let your mind terrorize your very existence.

It was then that I realized that it was not the seen or known fiend that frightened me, not now nor at any time in my life. What scared me the most is my clinging desperation to know my enemy in a sea of uncertainty. I feared the decay of order by my insistence to scratch at it. Leave it alone. Walk the edge sure, marvel mouth agape at the infinite, OK. But do not search for teeth and claws in this life unless you want to conjure them from nothingness. I felt pushed forward by the bloodthirsty playwright of time and it was my duty to clench down on the order like sands in my fingers for as long as I could bear it. And being confronted with that, looking straight down the barrel of the gun, I captured the dread that I was strangely craving. It was the opportunity to count my fears like the stars in the sky, loose track, mind dizzy and fall to the ground laughing at my minuscule, miraculously rare, impossibly stubborn life.

I snapped myself back to the moment, horn still beaconing me to come back. I grabbed hold of my imagined tether, and returned back to that purring 4-wheeler. My back was to the void now, the thick soup of probability teeming behind me, taunting me to look back over my shoulder and allow this moment of everything to collapse into something. But I refrained. Maybe it was the fear of seeing a charging elephant. Or the eeriness of blurred shapes across the hot dancing light of the horizon, halted with noses in the air. Maybe it was because I rejected my right to let this realm of the infinite collapse into one observed moment.

So I denied the abyss behind me and chose a brighter, more sensible path. I borrowed a pocket full of energy and slipped into that bubble that was my ride back home. Back to my camp under a hot tin roof and mosquito net, back to the familiar, to something preserved from bedlam. Ignoring the dark possibilities and content in the allusion of borrowed purpose. But still in decay, I would go about my days stalked by that old predator with teeth as sharp as time herself.

In truth, I am in no more danger today walking out my front door, confronting the infinite unknown, than I was staring across those vast high plains in Africa. And every single day I will continue to put feet to the floor, rolling dice on what collision course I have unknowingly set. But that day scanning the Serengeti plains is the one that haunts me still. It was the purest moment of surrender of my life; feeling engulfed and consumed by an everlasting void, frozen in time, disembodied and profoundly connected to nothingness and everything all at once.

"Like one, that on a lonesome road doth walk in fear and dread, and having once turned round walks on, and turns no more his head. Because he knows, a frightful fiend doth close behind him tread." - The Rime of the Ancient Mariner

Unleashed with Dogged Intent
a 'tail' of envious retreat

Have you ever seen an unleashed dog walking the sidewalk with all the authority of any other morning commuter? Your first thought will be to scan around for the owner. A dog without a leash is totally common in this neighborhood, but you'll want to see any manner of upright individuals minding their ward in this case. Responsible or negligent, it wouldn't matter, so long as someone drew a dotted line from a distance. You will look around for anyone keeping the same pace.

Then you'll look for someone trailing behind, hoping to sense someone on the same parallel trajectory, no matter how far back. Or to see someone far up ahead, slowing their pace, casting a cold eye over their shoulder, eventually stopping to give a whistle. Failing that, you'll even look for someone that matches the dog in style and stature. The pug faced lady, the shaggy brindle hippy, the lanky dover-black suited man. But there is no one tending to this hubristic hound, as he carves a parted sea through indifferent morning walkers.

A dog unleashed is one thing, unintended, slightly unsettling, you begin to find as you shift your weight around a cafe patio chair. Even if this quirky little quadruped had paused to sniff a post, lift a leg, or linger a bit with a cocked ear to all the bustle of the waking day, you could dismiss him as a stray. That small bit of pattern recognition would comfort you, remind you that all is working as intended, even if a bit chaotic.

But no, that boxy trotting boxer terrier never breaks his stride. Displaying all the intent and purpose of the rest of the surrounding upright mammals, high stepping their own way to work unattended. And for reasons you'll never understand, that unnerves you as much as if this conviction driven canine was suited up, walking on two legs himself.

As this pompous pooch makes his way to the end of the path, he pauses with the rest of the people at the large busy pedestrian walk. Paws sure footed, head pressed high, he perches petulant to the prying peers of the passersby, unperturbed in his pursuit.

And when the green man flashes, beckoning the large group to continue on, the vast majority veers to the left, dutifully chartered for their destination of tall office hives looming high overhead. But the untethered dog continues resolutely straight ahead down a quieter, narrower path. Your disquietude shifts from canine to man, as you ponder a new question. Which among these people envied most, if only momentarily, this unbridled vision of liberty, this dog's day unburdened by the intents of another, free to walk any path unleashed?

A Captain's Compass North,
a generational parable

The iceberg breaking hull was a master chef's knife, wasted and gliding deftly through calm, buttery arctic waters. Clouds were pulling themselves apart and winter's night sky constellations shone torchlights across scattered icebergs safely in the shadowy distance. This polar expedition passed quietly as the crew laid slumber and the captain handed over the night's watch to his first mate.

The young lad stood stewing at the bow, blood hot from an earlier disagreement at the evening's charter briefing. And as young lads do, he took it as personal assault that the old weathered captain overruled his course. Undermining him in front of the other officers, asking him to reserve his aggressively chartered course, given the icebergs. This spat had devolved into fiery tempers and defiance. Then it ended with the young man's dramatic denouncement of the captain's orders and his condescending advice disguised as restraint. He buttoned up his winter coat and stormed off to begin his nightwatch command.

The old captain bided his time to let the young lad cool his blood, before following him outside for a private conversation. And as old wise men tend to do, it was the captain that took the initiative, approaching his first mate at the ship's bow and making the first gesture of peace. They both leaned silent, elbow to elbow on the rail, as the captain pulled his ornate golden compass from a wool coat pocket and checked their bearings. The young lad folded his arms tight for warmth, closing himself off from the night. But he could not help to sneak a peek, seeking reassurance for his course. And then, with a gentle calloused hand on this young man's shoulder, the raspy old captain broke the silence.

"I'm not going to make you change your course. Bold as usual, but I trust we'll be safe. And it's not your brashness that I aim to tame, I hope you know. Only your stubborn insistence on being the smartest person in the room, no matter the advice. You say you prize free will and independence above all else. All the while, you deny the opportunity for guidance, help, or any surrender to providence. While you might be right most of the time, for you are after all a very capable sea skipper, you will never command the respect of your officers by going at everything alone. So I plead one last time for your attention.

"Look at this pretty old thing, this golden compass I've had since I was a cadet. There's a lot to be learned here about old school navigation, you know. Even more, there's wisdom here about fate. Consider for a moment, that this is you. That your whole body is an instrument, a compass. And what you call free will is the needle. You find comfort in, knowing your needle points in the right direction. You feel fulfilled knowing your vessel serves a purpose.

"Steadfast and reliable, always right, always there to serve you. Your purpose is self-contained, every answer you'll ever need, boxed inside you. And you feel in charge of the direction ahead. Confident in your ability to navigate your direction and your future, closed off from outside interference. A perfect, self-governing, self-calibrating golden compass.

"Now consider, what truly runs the compass. Is it you? Do you wind it, do you power it, do you maintain it? Does it not work on its own? But by what force of nature? Your will or something grander? I can see you know what I'm hinting at.

"We're chartered here on this bleak winter night, at our mighty ship's bow, deftly making our own way through the threatening icebergs. We're on our own in these harsh waters, are we not? Independently on the course, you've decided upon. And yet, looming overhead, regard the majesty of a clear open Arctic night sky. High above, watching over us. Ancient stars and glimmering planets clustering into patterns, secret maps of truth and whispers from our forefathers who deciphered them.

"And up in this dark blustery corner on Atlas' shoulders, now regard the northern lights, shimmering with electric greens and pinks. A sight of pure miracle and rare revelation? Or just a reminder of the magnetic field protecting us. And without that field, that golden compass of yours would point nowhere. Without the poles of the earth, there would be no purpose for your compass. It would be an empty vessel. There would be no draw, no pull, no meaning in the direction which that needle points.

"Can you see now, my son? Your own compass, this determination you so covet, it's an instrument of attraction towards something larger than yourself. It is the force outside the vessel that imbues us all with purpose and direction. It is the tent poles of the world that orient us. Guiding us, protecting us, reminding us of a higher force beyond our own egos.

"I can see you staring now at the lights, even if you will not look me in the eye. And I hope my words do not cause despair. This lesson should not cancel your free will or opportunity to seek a special and unique destiny. Especially for a capable man like you. He heard me correctly. Man, not boy, not any longer and I regret ever calling you otherwise. If you heed my advice, you'll find only a relief in not working to be so self-contained. So alone in your journey. Your mind, your intuition, your reason - they are all charged by something larger than us. Accepting that allows us to be more than a body. More than a vessel. More than the sum of our instruments.

"You are a good first mate, one of the finest. And someday you will be a better captain than me. But take heed not to allow self-reliance to corrupt itself into obstinance. Do not close out the underlying connection to the invisible whispers of the world. That would be like breaking the glass of this compass, and pushing the needle any which way you desire, then calling that north. This is not the point of free will.

"Understand this one truth, from a barnacled old man: free-will does not exist inside your small head, but is contained in the universal. When you accept that, you will learn to follow these intuitive nudges. These are the nudges entangled both in your will AND fate. And only when your mind is still and surrendered can you accept them. Put your faith neither in your determination nor in the stars, but rather, understand that they are wrapped up in each other.

"This is the wisdom of the sea and the heavens, my lad. Putting your faith here is not an abandonment of your ability. It is an acceptance that you are not just living in the world, but you are the world. Accept this, and you will have peace. And the way north will be clear and full of grace."

***

The captain took his leave but not before turning to place his own antique golden compass on the palm of the young man's hand. The young skipper could not deny that he had often coveted his mentor's prize compass, and would often wonder if it would be given someday as a present to his promotion to captain. His longing and eagerness faded quickly as he looked down at his palm and felt its heaviness. Heavier now than the sum of its parts. Heavy with the pull of the earth. He felt the pull of those invisible forces from the north, and for the first time felt connected to them, drawing him forward.

Pulling his wool peacoat a bit tiger against the westerly winds, this young night-watch commander felt the fear of icebergs and loss melt away, seeing a new illuminated channel opening before him. Clouds were waning to the prominence of Orion, Taurus and Gemini. The aurora borealis roared a burning beacon ahead. And an impossible gravity folded into this new captain's hand, pulling his anchored feet and the full ship with him north.

Was he doing the pulling, hand over hand like on a rope lassoed to the north pole? Was his anchored feet pulling the ship? Was the ship being pushed by the collective wills of the crew onboard? Was their destination a gravity well, locking the ship into an inevitable descent?

In this moment, the man did not measure the greater power, whether from the poles, from the tides, from the ship, from the crew, or from his outreached hand. It mattered not who was pulling whom, for it was all connected. The parting clouds now revealed a full snow moon, bathing him in white light. And the man never felt alone again.

Irish Fleets Wave Good Luck,
a post-lockdown Dublin

A fresh commotion was evident from outside your highrise window, overlooking the River Liffey. You make a fresh pot of coffee as the morning grows longer, and somehow sense, without looking, the stirrings of change. You take a glimpse outside with your hot mug in hand, and decide to put your morning Spotify atmosphere on hold. Instead you listen to the awakening below and for all signs that the world is moving on.

There was a TV crew next to your neighboring Irish naval ship, the W.B Yeats, moored to the south wall quay, having been there standing guard the past few months. All the officers were in their berets and ceremonial best, assembled on the foredeck for what looked to be a briefing. Along the river quay, a news anchor and cameraman were interviewing the older officers one at a time, including some emergency response members and An Garda officials.

Alongside them, a bagpipe player began sounding out some warmup blares. It wasn't unlikely during the past two months of this pandemic, that one ship might change guards for another, you think as the engines started up and pumped gray plumes into the air. But as you sweep your eyes down the South Wall, in this normally silent business district of Dublin, you see no sign of any other approaching vessel.

You rub the sleep from your eyes, trying to make sense of something different happening in these days of nothing new. You are surprised to see the block of emergency COVID testing tents, trucks and workers, had been packed up and disbanded early this morning. They had been there since the week of St. Patrick's Day, with clockwork efficiency just as Dublin's quarantine began. And for some reason, when you look at the now vacant sidewalks, without full context or understanding, you can't help but feel a little sad.

The lockdown is set to end this Monday the 18th, and Ireland seems to have fared better than most countries with strict adherence to the quarantine The navy had put together a strong show of support with their 'Operation Fortitude,' a three-port rotation of officer support and testing services across Dublin, Galway and Cork. You've seen the ships come and go in rotation before, but you feel certain this day;s departure marks the end of the mission.

The smoke keeps pumping from the *W.B. Yeat's* belly, as the crew stay busy, all hands on deck to say farewell. More and more response team workers start to arrive in yellow jackets, some with fire brigade kevlar, some with helmets, some with police hats. There is a fanfare and sentiment hanging heavy now, a large show of tribute to each of our frontline workers. Some pushing off, some staying behind, and all standing together in respect for each other.

The lines of the ship let loose and she began her mighty, majestic turn into the wide river, aiming her bow towards the distant rising Tom Clark bridge to the Dublin Bay. The Sam Becket bridge stands behind her, and you can almost imagine it's cabled harp strings playing along with the lone kilted man's pipes. The crew all stood at attention lined up across the rails, parallel to the local workers on shore, and reverent to the softly waving Irish flag on the aftdeck.

When the piper hit his final note, the crowd went silent for one perfect moment before ripping into applause. The crew waved, and you look around to see you're not alone on the balconies in this cluster of high rise flats, all of us self-isolated, many peering out and joining the moment. The sirens from the fire engines blaring, the people cheering the departure, striking a cord of much needed closure to the past few uncertain months.

As the '*Yates*' made her way to the toll bridge, still waving goodbye with green, white and orange, she let out three deafening horn bursts. This iron giant guardian was bidding her farewell, off to the open sea, with a firm reassurance to the good people of Dublin city.

"You'll be ok on your own now, we've all done our part together. You're in good hands here, but be sure to keep washing those hands. It's your time to look after each other."

You track her through binoculars and with your camera, as she fades into the distant horizon. The crowd disperses, the trucks move on, and we, the self-isolated, wander back into our homes.

A little confused, a little lonelier without the symbol of protection watching over us. During these uncertain times, the lockdown had been a thief of hope. But the departing crowd and waning fanfare, reminded you of the sidewalks bustling again with busy, determined commuters. And you felt the vibrance of purpose in that. Purpose that ushered in a renewal for hope with the shifting of a season, and the promise of a bright summer ahead.

Entangled States with an Irish Addict
a modern Dublin city noir

It can be a strange chain of events that plunge you into someone else's struggles. The late spring days of our quarantine were turning over to whispers of a much needed summer. And even though lockdown was easing, you find yourself stalling on a rainy day from pushing out the day. It's that old familiar crossroads you face almost every day this year, one between making an effort and hitting the *'feck it'* button. A routine week passes, sandwiched between two empty weekends that felt mostly the same in every way but their name. The highs and the lows, only measured by your ability to cut and paste from prior days routines. From good exercise in your spare bedroom, to no exercise. From Zoom calls and family chats, to only the lifeless face-masked courtesies at the local store. Bursts of motivation, followed by days of lazier needs. Netflix, bike delivered Indian curry, and oh hell, why not, add some overpriced beer cans to the order.

You can only take so much of this downtown before your body buzzes like a puppy to be let outdoors. Fine, why not. Anything different to mark the Tuesday. Anything to shake off the hangover, to self-sooth. To forget this soul sucking lockdown.

You consider yourself superhuman, a skilled drinker, better than most. You missed the buzzy mess of a late night crowd causing trouble past four in the morning on Harcourt street. But you also consider yourself a solo artist, more resilient than some to boredom or loneliness. You should have better odds of thriving amidst these dark days. Good survival skills, easily entertained, and a unique ability to bounce back.

But as your pounding headache grows louder, your survival instincts tell you its time to shake off the filth of another day almost wasted. You should probably try recovering by sweating out the stank in your tiny home gym, preparing a healthy dinner, pulling yourself up by the bootstraps and starting over.

Alas, the 'feck it' button blinks steady under hand. This little funk will clearly carry over an extra day, and you find yourself working to make a modified plan that serves both the need to be lazy and the need to be in motion. An instinct to forage kicks in, and you find yourself hungry. Finally, purpose! A reason to push off the couch. Part of the debate involves how to juggle a modest evening meal, and some small indulgence, like a glass of wine, to make it worth your while. Something classy maybe to dress up this waning day. Maybe a classy movie, a documentary, something to wash away the superheroes and tiger kings. Anything to mark this as *'a day that happened.'*

You resist the urge to order delivery, no easy routes here. But no overburdening yourself with too much cooking either. You settle on the compromise to put on some jeans, lace up some runners and push outside to the corner store. Maybe a small charcuterie snack, some aged Irish cheddar, a frozen pizza. You didn't promise this would be healthy, just not indulgent. Oh hell and why not a reward for being outside. Treat yourself to that top shelf bottle of Rioja they keep tucked away in the corner. Fifteen minutes there if you take your longboard, there and back again. Back to comfort, safety, and the sweet hum of your gigantic television.

It's funny how you can convince yourself on what passes for a well crafted plan. And how standards keep dropping in the desperation clouding around this quarantine. You've read this is what seems to be what happens to addicts, gamblers and gamers, drunks and meth heads. Your baseline of normal keeps shifting a little without you realizing. And like the earth turning under your feet, a few years go by, and you can't even trust your own orientation to remember which way you were facing yesterday. Yet here you are, your new normal, baseline fading, your compass spinning wild.

These thoughts flash together while skating up to the Spar, and like a summons from the cosmos, you spot the neighborhood beggar in her usual spot. Beggar? Sorry, drifter? Vagabond? Inhoused? Not even sure anymore. Let's just say she was in need. Relatively new on this beat, seemingly having migrated over from a different neighborhood, trying her luck on a more disposably wealthy crowd of the Grand Canal. She was a petite young Irish girl in her twenties, likely a rough sleeper based on her stained layers of tattered clothing. And almost definitely addicted to meth, based on her gray jagged teeth. Huddled in the damp like a shivering fox, she folded her legs across a soggy piece of cardboard along the sidewalk. And her image of quiet desperation reflected your own disquietude.

Through her grungy haze, you could still see she was very sweet and polite. A soft house mouse demeanor, always quietly reading a magazine under her worn hoodie, peaking out pursed lips to smile with warm gratitude to anyone sparing a coin for her cup. And although these fast walk-by exchanges were all you had known of her, it was on this day, this particular day when you barely made it out the door, that you were invited further into her world.

You enter the store, tip-toeing zigzagged past all the other shoppers, socially distanced, to the wine section on the back wall. Just then, a heavy commotion came swelling up from behind. Whipping around you notice the store clerk paused in his checkout process, with a fixed gaze over your head. The homeless girl had scuttled almost unnoticed past you. She darted around the end of the aisle, and cowered to a crouch on the floor. She pretends to flip through her bag, but it's clear she was stalling for time, as the clerk approached and asked what she was doing. She simply whispered, *"I just need a minute, I'll buy something, I swear."* It feels tense, and something was wrong.

You linger feeling a bit nosey, and quite frankly interest piqued from the drama, before shaking it off. Red wine, faux chic snacks, and an impulse bag of crisps in hand, you head to check out. The clerk was ringing you up, still distracted and looking past you. Clearly was an unusual turn for his sidewalk tenant, even in these strange days. As you walk outside the chain of events unfolds to you a little clearer. Pacing around just out the door were two gang clad, track suited characters, straight out of a Guy Ritchie movie. A man and a woman in their forties, the man in gold chains, the woman clicking bejeweled nails on her glittered mobile. She was wearing loud velour and silver studded black boots, with a buzzed haircut dyed red. The man had a scruffy chubby face, prison-style neck tattoos, and was clearly heavy out of breath from jogging.

You avert your eyes and brush shoulders past. They ignore you, shifting their weight impatiently. You look down at your skateboard, you look at your path home, you look back behind you. And you decide you couldn't leave, not just yet. It seemed dangerous, and you were no hero, but you compromised by posting up across the street on a park bench along the water, pretending to check your phone.

Now you recall seeing these thugs milling around earlier. How could you forget, this pair, so clearly out of place in this tech bubble neighborhood for young professionals. These 'Silicon Docks' were off-limits for their species of animal, but not so far away from their territory. The gangs from Sheriff Street tend to stick to the North and East Wall, so god knows what caused them to come hunting here. Maybe something about a pandemic, a city on lockdown and empty streets that brought all the wolves to sniff about for the wounded.

You feel affected, responsible, dizzy with adrenaline, and absolutely paralyzed with indecision. There was a new gravity in your day, and it sunk you onto that park bench immobilized. But what could you do, how could you get involved? More importantly, why should you? You make a balance sheet in your mind of options, pros and cons, risks versus rewards. Your rational mind quickly kicks in, screaming, pleading with you, *"This is not an action movie, you are NOT the protagonist of this story!"* And still you sat, glued to the scene, frozen and observing. Terrified for that poor sweet girl, ducking and huddled inside. Grasping for safety.

The apish man got his whispered orders from the woman on the phone, and eventually marched inside. Then out again shrugging his hands. He repeated this several times, each time not making a scene, knowing not to attract attention as he scouted about. Each failed attempt, had his handler pausing from the phone and berating him, mouthing words that sounded like, *"How much cash did she say she had? Can you get her outside? Any trouble from the staff?"*

It's clear through the open doors, the clerks were pacing about, aware of the situation but not actively trying to usher the girl outside. And the sinister duo just waited it out, patiently ready to collect some sort of debt. Stalking this poor mouse who so unwittingly had them on her heels.

Surely the shopkeepers would be calling the Garda by now. Or maybe this was your chance to help. But what would you say, would this even register? Maybe you could build your case first, observe and document any real threat. Investigate like you see so often on TV. The 'journalist's instinct' to be bold and wedge yourself into the story. Like those guerilla documentarians or those protesting activists. You always admired their determination to scratch at people's skin, no matter how disruptive and unpopular it made them. The sense of justice to go with your gut.

Today, you'd find you just don't seem to have that instinct. And that's probably for the better. You settle deeper on the bench, watching these despicable predators going about what animals do. And then common sense gets the better of you, like so many everyday folk in these times of retraction and self-preservation. You resign to fading away into the background. Perhaps if only to be here as a witness if it was needed later.

Does the world need real-life vigilante justice? Were you just making excuses for not at least speaking up, standing your ground as your basic human right? The one thing you knew for sure, justice aside, you felt a powerful and overwhelming compassion for this helpless cornered girl. Even though you knew very little about what led everyone here, it was pure compassion just the same. So you stand your ground, and continue to wait.

An hour went by, then another, without notice or disturbance. You feel locked into this triangle now and grow more stubborn by the minute. You even whisper to yourself that you would stay here all night if you had, if it meant making those tormentors have to endure a witness to their crimes. And just then, thankfully, it was the stalkers who threw their hands up first in defeat.

They made one last futile plunge into the store, a few whispered decisions on the sidewalk, and off they wandered, hopefully fucking off forever to their wolf den across the river. You would like to think based on their persistence that this was more than a money shakedown, more than just bored bullying. And you secretly hoped, vindictively, there would be a hard punishment from whomever they were returning to empty handed. But again, that's just too many mob shows and westerns in my head.

Not more than ten minutes later, the shivering hunched girl shuffled her feet to the entrance, peering shyly around the corner, a tiny desert mouse from her hole in the sand. At last, you feel a real chance to help, to follow your instinct. You break your cover and walk across the street towards her. She isn't startled, perhaps remembering your face from prior days. You point out the direction of her pursuers, so that she might head the other way, and ask if she needs your help. She declines and says she had somewhere to go.

On your way home, you remember skating here hours before, musing on the *entangled states* you shared with other desperate people. Addicts, gamblers, drunks, people lost in their fading baseline, sinking like quicksand. You think about fates being on a collision course that could never be foreseen. Then you think about those same people fading off into the future, into some new superposition of infinite uncertainties. Like this poor wounded soul, wandering just outside your field of vision, now out there swimming in a sea of possible outcomes, waiting for any new predator to spot her and for her fate to collapse again.

Perhaps it's best if you hadn't witnessed this event in the first place, making it a reality in your life. And perhaps not knowing what outcome awaits next for this girl, she'll stay suspended in the safety of an uncollapsed fate.

The next day you hoped to ignore the temptation to forget the events forever. Hoping to run into the same store clerks from the previous day, if only to ask for more detail. Hoping to understand the things you take for granted, shining a light on the dark forest of events, happening every day just out of sight. But tomorrow you will find no more insight, no more truth. The staff will be different and you will only find an empty, unoccupied spot of cardboard on the sidewalk outside. The troubled girl might be out seeking help, changing her routines, breaking her patterns, or being caught by new pursuers. She would be swimming around in that soup of the unknown.

As for tonight, on this day, and for the first time in a really long time, you bring home a bottle of wine that you don't even open, previously having chased the impulse to feel something on an otherwise nothing day. You bring home that fine red bottle and put it aside for a different rainy day. Afterall, you fulfilled your wish, your fix for the day, a day that did not pass unnoticed. You briefly shared a fate with this troubled addict, both trying to make our way back into the light. Finding cause to stand up for each other. And sharing each other's burdens like a good community should.

The Matrix of Living Abroad
a small island simulation theory

Like a shadow in your mind... there's always been that feeling that something was just a little off with this small pocket universe you're living in across the pond. Life in Dublin feels like a bubble of your life in D.C. everything is just a little different... a little stranger. It often feels like someone is trying to recreate how you think life should be here, and they took a few shortcuts to keep things simple. So you dwell a bit on simulation theory, and the idea that someone has programmed this whole thing for your benefit.

In fact, simulacra would be a more accurate depiction, because this feels less like a simulation of real-life events, and more like a copied depiction of things that don't really exist. Like the Truman Show or the Matrix, or a game of SIMs, you find yourself looking deeper down the rabbit hole and finding more and more emerging themes too common not to force some question about your new reality. Here's just a few that come to mind:

A replacement director changed the cinematography. There's drab design in the corporate buildings all around your neighborhood, lego blocks and glass panes, stacked up in a hurry during the big tech boom here on Grand Canal. The stark Irish haziness muddles everything into a soft hue and blurred edges. It's like you've turned your T.V. tinting down into a green, less saturated picture. Maybe it's just the constant cloud cover, but even on those cloud-breaking sunny days, it feels like a short term burst of programmable happiness, coded, not spontaneous. Perhaps it's a coincidence that when you travel back to the States, it's usually for summer or to Florida, but you are overwhelmed in those moments with the contrasting vibrant burst of saturated color. And it makes you wonder what worlds you just traveled between. And who stepped in to do the color grading on the Irish one?

An alternate universe would look like this. It can probably be attributed to culture shock, but there's just something about living in Europe that makes you feel like you've branched over to some parallel world. The world as you know it is familiar, but just a little different. The signs are different colors and shapes, the cash in your wallet is too. The grocery stores are logically in order, but still disorientating. The people speak English but it's not the same, like you're in a different time period - different accents, different slang and different contextual jokes. Hell they even drive on a mirror side of the road, how glitchy is that?! This is either a quantum leap, I've made somewhere else in space and time or some attempt to reprogram a different model reality.

The little programmed routines are everywhere. The routines and behaviors are so clockwork and predictable, it feels like someone wrote a lazy algorithm to keep it simple. Unlike the US, you don't see busyness all around you, random traffic jams, and frantic pedestrians criss-crossing the sidewalks. You see them on their scheduled routes, cars and people only during commuter hours, and then this business district completely empties out into a ghost town on the weekends. It dawns on you hauntingly, looking down from your high rise office or apartment, the sparse peppering of tiny sidewalkers feeling like automatons or video game NPC's. And you often wonder when you walk out from your neighborhood into the city-center, are new actors being rushed out onto empty streets? Does the map render as you walk? Do the characters?

There is no escaping the Island. This small ecosphere of Ireland that has become your entire world for months at a time, has managed parameters with tight corners and hard boundaries. Could it be a holodeck on a space station or an alien ship? Could it be a bubble studio set scripted and cast for you alone as the protagonist? Could it be a virtual world you're plugged into and immersed in, disembodied and fully deceived? The realization here is that this landscape, this island, would make for a very simple and manageable MMORPG. You're surrounded by a map that requires very little maintenance. You can't really drive endlessly in one direction, you haven't tried to sail across the channel. And any trips you've taken off of Ireland have been well planned to the same airport, that portal that usually involves extensive screening, some numbing agent cocktails, and often a nap. One wonders, are you really flying out of Ireland, or is it some other data exchange?

The physics and relativity just feel off. Space and time just feel different when you come back to America. Some of it is explainable, like the jet lag from time zones, etc. Some of it is more bizarre, like how you always run at a much higher pace, minutes per mile, in the States, setting new personal bests with lower effort. It's almost as if your programmers (aka, machine overlords) couldn't quite write the equivalent code for space time here in Ireland. You find yourself in touch with friends at a 5 to 8 hour time difference, and they're always experiencing a different part of the day. You have no concrete proof that you're not just calling them from inside a pocket universe that has no time at all, being allowed to connect with the real world in order to maintain the charade.

And so... you sit and you linger on the probabilities. The unknowable truths. You ruminate a minute more and you draw what conclusions you can. What could they be? What can you say for sure? Well, those you should keep to yourself, those you should not say out loud. For you never can quite be sure who or what is here listening. Notice it, sure. Dwell on

it, ok, but not for too long. Question it, never. Because, let us all agree…
the Guinness here, in this reality, is far too delicious, and there's always a
few women in red dresses fluttering about.

Epilogue: Reflections, *the more personal essays*

The Octagon, *lessons from my father*

Part I. What brings you here.

I've heard it said that man's salvation is in picking up God's graces. And grace comes from art. And art does not come easily.

Growing up, this was made clear to me by my father through the art of golf. I believe that he saw golf as more than a sport but rather a life philosophy. And from an early age, some of my best time spent with him was going to the local driving range and receiving instruction on my swing. As I understood it, a perfect golf swing required the rhythm of a concert pianist and the clarity of a Buddhist yogi. And the inherent human flaws in a golf swing were a true indication of the level of balance in your mind. Subsequently, you could tell how well a man's life is by the way he's swinging his golf club. So I practiced this meditation over and over again as a boy, sometimes taking as many as five, ten, or twenty practice-swings before even stepping up to a ball.

Despite my early start in the game; I should admit that I am now, at twenty-eight, a pretty awful golfer. It's an irony that often haunts me but I don't yet regret. I used to think that my father's stern instruction kept me from enjoying the game because it felt more like homework than sport. In truth, my father's respect for the game was so high that going to the driving range was really the bulk of my experience in the game. I never stepped foot on an actual course until I was twenty-one years old. Even then, I didn't feel like I deserved to be there. There was still a tick in my swing that I could never seem to shake. Something in my life that reared its ugly 'sliced' head in a really embarrassing fashion. So it seemed irreverent for me to bring it on to the golf course, my father's church.

And yet still today, I play golf. Rarely as frustrated as you're tempted to be, ever curious about the secret mysteries of the perfect swing. Some seasons, I play a round as few as one to two times. But in true form and respect for the game, I often found myself making time for the driving range. My silent step outside myself. My inquiry into the balance in my life.

Part II. Taking Stock

On one particular day in such inquiry, I found myself in a curiously lost state of mind. I felt a warning imbalance and my future seemed uncertain. The cause of my duress was a career shift I was trying hard to take on. After close to seven years of sales experience, I had managed to lay down the foundation for the skills I had hoped to achieve as a businessman. And as I stood solid on this foundation, I found that the opportunity to keep building was far too great to stand still for even a moment.

So I took a chance and spent more time looking beyond my current role. Taking interviews to see what my experience was really worth, an appraisal of sorts of the early stages of my experience. Not knowing what was out there or where it could take me, I cast my line and I hoped. What I pulled back was a bounty that I didn't expect. It started with one company and multiplied quickly to many. If I was looking for any validation in my profession, I got it back tenfold. I got the message, loud and clear from the world, and ultimately drew one conclusion. Aim higher.

Three months, thirteen companies, and eighteen interviews later; one company emerged as a clear match. I had seen jobs that I was overqualified for that didn't want me. I had seen jobs that I was under-qualified for that wanted me bad. And I had seen a lot of combinations of bad luck and bad timing in between. But I came out of the process with an understanding of what my next step should be. And I saw that step in a medical device market leader, a company that would be the envy of my peers. My championship trophy.

And I had cleared three of the four stages of their quote thorough interviews already. Now, I just waited for the phone call that would arrange for the final test, an invitation to fly to their headquarters to meet the big boss. And from there, I was a shoe in.

But in the meantime, I was on pins and needles, waiting for the horizon to hit my tires. Waiting, because that's all I could do.

Part III. Seeking Answers

Being one of the first beautiful days of an early Washington, D.C. spring, it was clear to me how I could find my sanctuary from this anxiety, although I wasn't clear on where. I needed to find a close-by driving range and gain some insight into what was really going on in my head. The trouble was that the closest one to me was closed for renovations, and several others that I knew of were a little too far outside the beltway for my present disquietude. But I took a chance that a local nine-hole public course would have at least a modest area set aside to warm up my swing.

I drove there with my moon-roof exposed, music filling my soul and glorious sunshine splashing off my Ray-Bans. I was edging my way towards peace. When I got there, however, I was disappointed to find that this golf course didn't have the traditional driving range I was hoping for. Set off from the clubhouse, there was a narrow gravel path leading to five stations, each with a green mat and a chewed up rubber tee, separated by four short, rusted gates and all enclosed by a big-top tent of a screened net for you to hit your balls into. It was a pathetic sight. What I really wanted was an open field to see the flight of my ball. Today more than ever, I needed to know where the ball was heading: how bad my slice was and whether it could be tamed.

But being that I had already come this far and my hunger to loosen up my body and mind was so great, I decided that this would have to do. So I ponied up to the clubhouse and came out with a large bucket of beat up, rejected golf balls. I walked down the gravel path to the last spot in the row, away from the world. It was the middle of the day on a Thursday, so no one was really there. And once I settled into my station, I rediscovered the beauty of the sunkissed spring day as I stretched a seven iron across my back, calmed my mind and breathed purposefully again.

As I stepped up onto my mat to where I had set my bucket by the tee, I looked down at this thick foam platform and noticed its corners were cut equally into eight sides. I was intrigued to notice how perfectly it lay centered in the flat-square plane of concrete that was my area. And so there I was, residing in my small concrete universe, standing upon my tiny little octagon world, looking outward and about to begin a very simple meditation.

Part IV. Outside the Octagon

The first stroke came down hard on the top of the ball and sent it sailing low to the bottom right corner of the net. It bumped the net with a weak blow. The second shot came off a little cleaner but still didn't feel right. It sailed to the right and smacked the net with a deep thud. The third was about the same. Not exactly the best start I could hope for. And I was frustrated already, mostly at the arena that I had chosen. If only I could see where the ball was going. I needed to know how far I was hitting it, how bad it was slicing right. I needed to see the results, although I had an idea of what they would reveal.

I had topped the ball severely on the first shot and it had sent a bad vibration up my arms to warn me about my rhythm. I left my club face open on the other two and knew it by how awkward and naked my swing felt on the downstroke. I could feel what was going wrong but for some reason still wanted the proof. And then I did something on the next swing. I told the net to go away. And with a wave of my hand, it did. It folded itself up and revealed an open lane just for me. I painted this fairway a bristled green, opening it wide on both sides and extending it to the warm blue horizon. I was a child again, looking outward and anxious for validation of my efforts. I lined up my stance and relaxed my grip a bit, getting ready to swing.

Controlling the tempo, I drew my club high above my head, preparing to strike. But then something unnerving and familiar happened. I took my eye off the ball for an instant to sneak a peek at my imagined fairway. It was a quick glance, but in that instant my whole world crumbled. My only wish was to keep the ball from slicing off the fairway. But the more I thought of it, the more this once wide fairway incurved like a dented mirror. And it continued to bend inwards until the only thing left was a bike trail of a narrow green target. I plundered down hard on the ball, almost missing it completely, and shanked it so hard right that it pinged the corner of the rusted gate divider. Net or no net, I knew exactly where that shot went.

Part V. What's Inside

Then something occurred to me. What results am I seeking? What do I need to know that I don't know already? And most importantly, what do I care what happens outside this octagon? Once the ball leaves this area, I've already done everything I could possibly do. And if I focus too strongly on the target, that target only gets smaller and harder to hit. So what should I think about, what can I control? I can control my rhythm. I can think about my grip, the weight of the clubhead as it swings into its pendulum, the way I rotate my wrist coming down. I can think about how it feels when I hit the ball and how I did sending it outside the octagon. After that, I've done my job. The rest is up to the world.

I breathed slowly. I stayed focused on what was close to me. And I took my swing, thinking only about how it felt, not what happened next. Instantly, I knew what felt wrong and I knew what I wanted to change. It wasn't really something specific, just a different feeling I wanted to get out of hitting the thing. So I pulled another ball to me, breathed deep again, and I hit the damn thing. This time I got the feeling I wanted. So I hit another, and another, and another, each time getting the feeling I wanted from the strike. I changed clubs and continued my meditation, letting nothing outside my octagon interfere with the actions I knew to be right. And I knew them to be right, not because I saw how they played out, but because I could feel it. Down to my bones, I knew what was right... on feel and on faith.

As I kept myself centered in the octagon, I found something else besides the tools at hand. There was an answer to the question I had asked by coming here. The question was 'what will become of my interviews and eventually my career?' And the answer became 'who cares, it's outside your octagon'. What I knew, and what I could feel is that, centered in the moment of the interview, I performed to my potential. My mind was clear and my words felt right when I sent them off into the world. And the rest, is up to the world.

It's not necessarily the strongest way to sooth the anxiety of what's to come. But it helps to understand that when the next moment arrives for me to perform, I'll stay focused in my octagon, unclouded by the things outside my control. It's a faith of dedication. It's a meditation that keeps me encouraged by the uncertain yet oncoming future.

Part VI. Taking it with you

As I finished off a satisfying bucket of golf balls, I took my final swing with a driver. The rhythm made my soul sing and the whoosh that followed perked my ears. It was a perfect swing. And I knew it without any proof. But the devil inside me, had me sneak one quick peek at the result. Out of the corner of my eye I saw the ball smack hard at the top dead center of the net. As I turned on my heels to leave, I stepped off my platform and smiled as I indulged the fantasy of the net dropping and allowing my ball to sail to its beautiful warm blue horizon.

And although I left that eight-sided green platform behind me, I feel it beneath me now as I get ready for my final interview. Will I get the job? How will my message be received? What's my destiny? How do people see me? Are my words too harsh? Are my intentions understood? Will I sink this putt? Will I hit my target? Will I find my way home? Will I be the man I desire to be?

I'll take the answers on faith... but they're all outside my octagon. And most of the time it's up to the world. Inside my octagon, is a man with leather soles and high ambitions sending out big ripples across the world - listening patiently for the echoback. What's in yours?

Around the Lake's Bend, My Father Goes
an essay on grief and loss

I'll always remember the last time I got Dad into a kayak. I was home in Rochester from Ireland risking a visit to see my parents just this last September. The lockdown had been grim enough already on the emerald island, but the real kick in the teeth was that any semblance of summer weather days had skipped over us entirely this year. I had been nostalgic for Fall in upstate New York, so imagine my delight when I got the best of both worlds for my visit: the autumnal turning of the leaves and a warm sunny Indian summer!

My parents and I shared a lot of adventures during this time. We took Sunday drives around the Genesee canal, sat around campfires, ate Bill Grays cheeseburgers, & visited country stores in search of the perfect pumpkin pie. We even rented a place up on Fourth Lake in the majesty of the Adirondack Mountains, in homage to our many family trips to Raquette Lake. The sunny days were perfect as we toured the local Hardware Store of Old Forge, and the great American diners of a lost world. Those days faded too quickly, like the golden autumnal sunset dipping across a burnt sienna horizon, as we toasted our happy hour cocktails at the splashing loons from our lakeside Adirondack chairs.

The weeks spent together, from Adirondacks and back to Rochester, were full of fond memories like these, streaks of nostalgia stoking the fires along with the forging of new memories together. But by far the time I remember most, was the drive I took with dad to Casey Park, Ontario, on my birthday. We jerry-rigged his kayak to his open trunk, although Dad played coy about whether he would use it himself. Always the delegator of tasks, I think he just wanted to watch me using it and being happy in this peaceful small lake oasis that had always been his private little paradise. We listened to triumphantly drumming symphonies on the drive out and as I got the kayak out, Dad bellowed out his rendition of Happy Birthday, before cracking open a small ceremonial airplane bottle of bourbon to share. He told me to take my time and enjoy the paddling, while he sat dockside fishing meditatively. I had a great commune with nature on that stretch of water, snapping photos along the way of sunbathing turtles and mighty gray herons. I could see the peace of this park coming to life with every emerging color-pop, and a kaleidoscopic overhang of maple leafs.

On my return to the dock, my dad started to beam at me and seemed to project that he wanted his turn now, not content to allow this moment pass by as a mere vicarious one. And said, "maybe I'll give it a try if you think you can hoist me in." His hips had become so frail through the years, his steps were small, his body always teetering. I was nervous at first but feigned confidence so that he would surrender his trust. I helped him sit at the edge and swing his legs down to the mooring spot, we got his life jacket on and stood him up behind the kayak. I came behind him and gave him a solid bear-hug to hoist him off the ground. My dad felt lighter than I expected and went still like a doll. I felt the rough skin of his face on my neck, and his quietness as he held his breath with a twinge of pain and expectancy. I dropped him in with ease, and with a push he was gliding off into his perfect paradise.

I stood and watched him head off for his own adventure, paddling lightly, no longer hindered by his fragility, coasting along with ease. He would only look back once to wave. He would pause often looking off pensively along the water's edge. He would hoot and holler with joy. And then he would round the small lake's bend, and disappear into his own eternal wilderness. I am overwhelmed now at this memory, filled with joy, sadness, grief and celebration. And I am haunted by the majestic beauty of these waters, as they continue to whisper the music of my father.

Dishwashing and All That Jazz,
reflections in mourning

You wait to choose your moment perfectly. The timing is critical around this dinner table. The excitement of your family gathering charges everyone up. The booze from happy hour intensifies the joy and the red-faced storytellers around the room. The energy carries over into a celebratory dinner, moments of raised wine glasses, praises to the chefs, stories, debates, and even some softer sentiments... words of remembrance for your recently passed father. This is why you're here, back home where you began in Rochester, NY, sharing your time, reconnecting with immediate family. The days have turned into weeks as you all heal and grieve together. Sadness gives way to fondness, and disorientation gives way to your roots in family gathering. The celebrations continue each day, big and small. Sometimes in the small family cell around the Carreo family table of your youth. Sometimes out to dinner, using your shared grief as an excuse to pause on pandemic caution. Sometimes with your extended family and Rochester remaining cousins. Each time a little different, each time a little familiar.

Tonight, you are at your Uncle Bob and Aunt Janet's home, a warm home, a family familiar one from your childhood. It's your mom's big brother, and they shared a great fondness for your dad, offering the richest stories and sentiments to fill the hole in your heart. There is magic here and connection, and somehow the whole night feels continuous with the nights before. You can predict the energies, the stories told, and who the spotlight will turn to next. You know your own part to play, your waxing and waning spotlight as you shift from regaling story teller to curious listener.

And as the dinner table starts to exhale deeply into a calm sigh, you sense a few crossroads. Either someone claims the next spotlight, as you sink deeper into your chair, losing your attention span and retreating to your quiet recharge mode. Or we all snap into busy bee mode simultaneously, scrambling to collect dishes, dueling politeness with insistence to help, as we arm wrestle over each other in a small kitchen to all lend a hand, preferring to stay in motion over being the odd man out. Or you devise a third option, and play the room like a poker table. You strike first, careful not to choose the wrong moment, too soon or too late. Careful not to invite chaos or discordant politeness. Confident enough to set a course that all could follow.

You push back from the table, with both hands flat down, and say strongly, "I would like to clear, please, stay seated and keep talking, I won't do much". The small hesitations, the stuttered resistance, and then a wash of relief from our hosts to say, "Ok, but don't clean up too much, we'll serve dessert soon."

This is where you shine, this is when you feel most at ease. An opportunity to take a break from the loud energy, a chance to recharge with busy work on your own and without retreating to introversion. A chance to offer service and kindness to keep a better relaxed harmony at the table. Naturally, you do more than you explain, but the ruse was well played. You bring the stack of plates around the back doors of the kitchen, you turn up Alexa's jazz playlist loud... partly to muffle the loud clanking pots and pans, and partly to give yourself a playlist while you jam away, dancing your dance of labor.

And you recall all the times when you've been in this exact same position with your family. The night before even with your dad's sister's family. Two nights before with your sister Julie's and husband Adam's gourmet cooking. One week ago, my sister Jennie's family nestled around our old family Carreo table. Last Christmas, with Mom and Dad alone. Two summers ago, after a large family sunny deck party at our house. And backwards through time until you can remember, before even the summer job as a busboy and pan scrubber at Hedge's restaurant, on your feet every night, sweating it out for under-the-table beer money. Those upstate NY summer nights working at this fine dining lakefront establishment were formative, watching each night as that grand restaurant came alive with candlelight, live piano jazz and special dinner guests crowding the bar and dance floor before being seated to their special dinner table, their own perfect moment.

Each night there was a swell of magic, ambiance, connection and fleeting pursuits of joy. Each night, there was that slow wind down, dispersion, scramble to close and clean up. And each night, you marveled to watch this shift, as you shifted from the early night boisterous engagement to the quieter times scrubbing those pots and pans.

This is how it's been ever since, and this is where you find your personal retreat. Your chance to show gratitude for the evening, the many hands that brought food to our table, near and far. The chance to contribute in some meaningful way, in your presence, but also in your conducting harmony at the table, so that those involved may enjoy each other's presence.

Before you know it, you're getting hollered to come back to the table and share the dessert. You snap out of your jazz induced trance, and look around to find the dishwasher fully loaded and cookware all stacked and rinsed. You may have done too much, maybe you lingered too long, but you rejoin the table with a revived energy and raise one more glass. We sit together joyously at this table, and you feel the time warping around it, as if it is every table you've ever known to be with family and friends. You feel the presence of each personality, the many hands, the thousand smiles. And in that moment, you see the face of your father sitting right beside you, smiling deeply, and here with you today and all the days forward.

Stranger Dangers & Tickle Fights, *sick family pranks*

It's unfathomable to think not every person gets the uncontrollable urge to tickle a sullen Japanese businessman staring woefully out across the river's edge. That common scenario has never presented itself to you? Well, here's some advice for when it does. You certainly don't have to act on that urge. In fact, assuming he is a stranger and having a private moment, it's almost almost best that you do not. However, to deny its urge in the moment, to insert yourself into someone's extremely private moment of reflection? Well, forgive me, but I think you might be lying to yourself.

Imagine it now. There you are, going for a nice walk on a gloomy overcast day along Dublin's River Liffey. There are scattered pedestrians around, perhaps just stretching their legs from their prolonged home office sittings. Perhaps taking this break to smell something other than their roommate's laundry or their own breath under a constant unrelenting face mask.

You see all these people walking, some speeding along with a friend, some smoking a cigarette, some stumbling a little bit with a six-pack of cans swinging at their side. Before the lockdown, people walked with purpose on city sidewalks, commuting in a rush, with the authority they had a grand quest to complete. Now we all seem to shuffle our feet with the air that we're killing time in the prison courtyard before our fateful return to the cellblock.

And that's why on my walk, I couldn't keep my eyes off this older Japanese man, looking so sullenly out across the water, barely walking at all. He moved his feet just enough not to tip over, like you would on a bicycle moving too slow. You have to wonder what existential dilemmas he could be pouring over? What solace a sad black suit wearing businessman would be taking from an Irish waterfront. Perhaps dreaming of his homeland on a similar shoreline, perhaps pondering why he moved here in the first place? And all you can do is think about rushing up to him in a startling way, yelling *boogada boogada boogada*, and tickling him to an uncontrollable laughter. Then just walking away without explanation.

Perhaps you don't understand this feeling, in which case, you probably don't have a sister like mine. My older sister Julie, has always been the one to provoke this type of lunacy. From her trouble making youth as the first-born golden child, she could get away with anything, troll any serious conversation, and prank anyone stupid enough to let their guard down in the family. My father for example was never safe from her surprise attacks to pull his pants down whenever he was getting a little too self-confident, and often in public. It's a wonder the man didn't lose his hair earlier, or at least double up on belts and suspenders. Or just never turn his back on his mischief daughter.

Julie's the kind of person that would ask the question with an impish grin pushed out by her twisted mischief brain, "How often to you every come across the opportunity to truly fuck with somebody like never before? I mean really shatter their sense of reality. Exactly, then why would you ever waste one?"

I think that's what she said verbatim the time I surprised her and her husband Adam with a trip down to their home in Florida. It was a last minute surprise for the weekend. But I was a rookie in the craft of surprise compared to Julie, and never thought through the best way to shock them into convulsions. It must be a recessive gene in me, because our younger sister, Jennie, has these mutant powers too. Jennie will often coyly keep all her family's travel plans a secret until the very last minute. Or until you find yourself being ambushed on a nice private loungey beach vacation, totally relaxed and ready to switch off, only to be attack-hugged by her two boys.

So I figured I had waited long enough to spring my surprise, lingering on decency and calling Julie after my flight to let her know I was in a cab to her house. To me, that was good enough notice, my big *'surprise'* reveal! *"I'm here now, and on my way! Did I surprise you? Good, see you soon."* Such an amateur. Julie would probably prefer that I made a little more of an effort. Popping out of an oversized box that I had FedExed to their place. Or pulling off a rubber mask while they were out to dinner to reveal I had been their waiter all night long. Again, not my strength. And you could feel her initial excitement slowly fade into slight disappointment as she tailed off, "Cool, see you soon."

At her doorstop, after hugs, you could tell she had been thinking about all the ways I *should've* surprised her instead. "Why didn't you surprise me at my door? You didn't have my new address? Maybe just text me for it, I wouldn't have asked why. Or found my superintendent and asked to be let into my place. That would've really scared me shitless!" I nodded away trying to move on, but she kept drafting more fake plans for me.

This wasn't going away anytime soon. There was opportunity in this mind game and her eyes kept darting around, as if I was a student interrupting my math professor, in the midst of her completing a high level proof at the chalkboard, waving off my unhelpful suggestions. Her eureka moment followed, as she remembered quite fortunately that her husband Adam was still at work. Now my arrival was merely a rehearsal for something truly terrible. And she relished this devilish plotting with the enthusiasm of a Bond villain stroking her cat in a swivel chair. This moment will be ours, she seemed to beam!

Our strange game was now afoot. Her master plan was for me to dress up in a hoodie and street clothes. She would get on the phone on his commute home and warn him that she saw some suspicious kids roaming around their parking lot and that the rental office had advised her to stay indoors until they called the police. Meanwhile, I would go out and run at him, while he was getting out of his car. Let's see if we can get this poor guy's heart rate up with some 'stranger danger,' Julie reveled.

If you knew my brother-in-law, you would realize immediately that this was a bad plan. Not just because it's, you know, a terrible thing to do to someone. But because he's not a demented sadist like the rest of my family! There was no victory to be had here, picking on someone that would never retaliate. Best case scenario, he'll likely jump startled, and then inevitably just ask, "Oh, it's just you. What's for dinner?" And as for the worst case scenario, you might ask? Probably some combination of us writhing around on the parking lot pavement, him having a heart attack, right after stabbing me with his keyring knife. Swell prank, Julie.

This seems to be the secret of their happy marriage, Julie gets free license to play her sick jokes, or twisted games of "Would you Rather" (horrific 'Sophie's choice' scenarios she conjures up, some which still make me shudder worse than any 'Saw' movie). Adam endures them all patiently with eye-rolls, as Julie asks, "Would you rather be tickle-tortured to death, or have to french kiss every person that says hello to you for the rest of your life?" Adam, just biding his time for her to wear herself out, so he can shift to topics more adult, like his favorite Youtube chefs or the upcoming NASA shuttle launch. Sometimes our late night Carreo family shenanigans can get interrupted with a *"I don't see why that's so funny."* This only reinforces our belief that the Carreo kids are part of an advanced tribe of comedy savants that would sooner translate Japanese to dolphins than to explain a joke.

Speaking of Japanese, back here in Dublin, I have now walked the southside banks of the river twice, been to the store, and completely lapped our Japanese friend in his daze of ennui. Mostly just shaking his head and mumbling to himself, maybe he was in fact speaking to dolphins. But more likely, he was ruminating over a bad conference call or some office politics that sent him over the edge. Watching his inner monologue playout visually was mesmerizing, and I almost preferred to abandon my tickle-attack impulse, in favor of just pulling up a bench, some snacks from my grocery bag, and enjoying the show. But I'll return to our little friend from the land of the rising sun a little later.

Back again in Florida, we're moving forward with 'project heart attack.' I was dubiously disguised in my hoodie and sunglasses, trusting in my sister's supreme sense for abstract humor (or was it terror). I dutifully marched outside to assume my role, baffled that her husband takes anything seriously she says at all anymore. On the other hand, Julie would call 'the boy who cried wolf' a goddamn amateur. Maybe it's because she's really dedicated herself to always dwelling on the macabre, honing her intuition for bullshit, and knowing how to side-step it deftly. Maybe it's because she's an honest to god doctor of neuropsychology, with a license to mindfuck more dangerous than the most devious of fabled mad scientists. Regardless, her plan proceeded masterfully.

I wasn't in the room, but I imagine her first phone call to Adam was worthy of an Emmy, not overacted, but offering the subtle hysteria of someone not thinking straight and needing a hero. I believe there was a series of these calls, as my dear trusting brother-in-law, probably pressing his foot harder to the accelerator, jacked up his stress meter to an already aggravating commute home. Julie was leading the scoreboard early on, a cat toying with her cornered prey with smug delight.

Her campaign continued, as he peeled into the complex, and I circled around the block. Now she was free-styling like an expert, baiting him with statements like, *"I'm just going to walk outside for a little bit to see if he's still there"*. He'd scream his protest and tell her not to move, *"Relax!"* he'd say, *"Stay put!"*, he'd yell. As she probably had to press her face to a pillow to keep from laughing.

I rounded the corner where I saw him walking, cell phone in hand. His pace slowed when he saw my character and folded his phone away. And as people tend to do, his confrontation aversion was kicking in, eyes dropping, his course veering ever so slightly away from me.

Well, I'm not Julie, but I know the moment of pay-off when I see it. So I mustered up my best hard-sell, and started charging him with an elaborately cartoonish arm-waving and freakish head-bobbing, which I was surely borrowing from my own childhood nightmares. I either looked like the attacking clown from Stephen King's It, or like Scooby Doo running in place from a ghost. Either way, it must've registered high on Adam's 'fight or flight' response because he immediately assumed a hovering, crouching Sumo position of readiness that I could only describe as tai-chi meets eighties's dance-fighting.

Picking up my charge as convincingly as I could, suddenly my own amygdala-jacked brain got some bizarre wave of confusion. *"Are we in a fight? Am I in danger? Should I tackle him? Is it now him or me? How the hell did I get talked into this?"*

I imagine all these thoughts going through both our simple caveman heads simultaneously, while an upstairs window curtain parted to reveal the smiling face of our puppetmaster Julie, savoring the play she so perfectly directed.

Realizing I had no plan for what was meant to come next, I stopped short and just started roaring with laughter. Out of breath and really throwing my head back, waiting for Adam to catch on. In his sudden clash with reality, he went through a very rapid sequence of reactions that flashed, *"What's happening? Who are you? Oh wait, what? It's you, you're here?"* And then, after catching his own breath simply, *"Oh god damn friggin Carreos!"*

As you can imagine, the rest of the evening was Julie trying to retroactively sell the brilliance of the gag back to Adam as his pulse settled down, and he nodded along blankly, so eagerly ready to move on, secretly knowing this wouldn't go away any time soon.

Back in Dublin thinking about this moment, a prank in my toolkit I briefly considered pulling out. I picture Julie on my shoulder egging me on. I think about the risk versus reward, and I wonder where it could go. There would be no build-up, no script to follow, not even a real punchline moment. I would run up and tickle this poor man in solitude, and then hope it would just occur to him I was only trying to make him laugh, you know, as a favor? Maybe? Perhaps not.

After the scare, maybe we would both throw our heads back and share a really good laugh, even if Adam didn't. Then he'd shake my hand, or bow to me, even thank me for taking him out of his own dismal head. He'd invite me over for dinner and we'd share delicious ancient family recipes, even some high reserve sake. In the end, I would become part of their family, and travel back with them to Okinawa, where I would help them restore their family dojo against their rival family dynasty. Maybe it would play out that way. In an alternate universe.

But I wouldn't find out in this one. Without an audience to play to, the effort to reward just wasn't there, so I had to shuffle past him.I would get no confused look, or wash of relief. I would get no laugh, nor a punch in the face. But through the wisdom of my sister Julie, the opportunity to plot and spread chaos, an absurdly twisted moment to amuse only myself, that was its own reward.

I imagined the business man's different reactions all the while walking home, watching his whole reality cracking in his confused face, and to me that would have been everything. Doing it or not doing it is about the same for me, because either way, it gave me a break from myself. That's the gem I hold onto every time I think about splashing some chaos onto somebody's day. That's the gift of absurdity that I learned from my older sister.

Don't Be An A**hole To Strangers
an essay on absurdity as a balm

This has been stewing for a while. It's a stew of anger, contempt, and entitlement packed into a dutch oven, swirling together in its own rich sauce. It's a stew approaching a point beyond infused blended flavor, into something inedible, something rank. It's a point of no return, where I descend into that salty curmudgeon of an old man, walking shaky, grimaced and fist balled at those irreverent kids all around me. It's the worrying unpleasant manifestation of my worst petulant self, defiant to everything wrong with my life and the society around me. It's my calcification into being an asshole to strangers. It's someone I don't wish to be.

I want to change, I desire it deeply. Cut the head off this one dragon before it grows into a hydra. I walk around Dublin in my self-reflective haze. I think about times before in this city, in many other cities across Europe, across the world; trodding about and stewing in my own muck. And I have a vague sense of when it began, not pinpointed, just a feeling. A slow creeping fog of being bothered, and the addictive grip of wanting to be bothered, wanting to maintain and validate the compulsion. Reinforcing it and looking wildly for the confirmation clues that infect me like dark radioactive material.

First, start collecting the triggers. *Those kids shouldn't be doing that. Those drunk ladies on their hen party look appalling and are acting obnoxious. That woman looks like a miserable cunt. This guy is about to cut me off in line. This neighborhood is disgusting.*

And then the extrapolations start. *Those kids are everything wrong about bad parents and lazy teachers (and it's only getting worse). That hen party is everything wrong with fashion, consumerism and a social media driven self-absorption. This woman needs to be put in her place. This guy is my competition, stiffen up and edge him out! This neighborhood is a sign of the housing crisis and the greed of man that makes my life difficult. Arghhh, bark, growl!!*

Too many voices in my head, too many triggers that disrupt my calm. My stroll, my vacation, my chance for self-reflection and peace of mind… spoiled. What's more, I was beginning to make my identity wrapped in this entitled notion that it was my right, no, my duty, my whole reason for being to march around and teach strangers some manners. One city wander at a time, one passive aggressive comment at a time. That will put everyone in their place, right? That's what will balm my inflamed ego. Except it doesn't. Counterintuitively, it only makes the world around me uglier and my calm further out of reach. It's all total bullshit and it needs to stop.

So I try a new tactic. I make a choice. I decide to let everything play out and smile at it. I allow everyone their lane, and I offer no judgment. When I feel myself tense up with an observation, or a sneer, I diffuse it with a smile as if I just saw something wonderfully unique I may never see again. I focus hard to ensure I'm not just smiling with false bravado, but as a gentle reminder that this intrusion can not hurt me. Chuckling quietly also seems to work, so long as I'm not allowing someone to feel disrespected. That only serves my own ego and is a ploy for dominance over others. Let that go. After all, there is a delicious delight to be had in absurdism, if I keep an eye out for the comedy playing out all around us.

Here is where I realize no one can rob my peace because it comes from a place of emergent self-esteem. And that state is no man's charter but my own.

This won't be easy to maintain, emotions get heated, people get ugly. People can rob me of my time or make things more difficult. There are reminders of a broken system and chaos all around me, I don't have to bury my head in the sand over that. But it doesn't have to steal my peace. Push past me in line and make me late, fine. Be a terrible person in your own life, that's your choice isn't it. Remind me of the starving children in Africa, it's terrible, yes. And if you're genuinely being an asshole to me, I'll let you feel like 'the big man'. It is absolutely no skin off me. I'll smile and soldier on with my own prerogatives. I'll give myself fifteen minutes extra time to get to where I'm going. I'll assume good intent with someone having a bad day. I'll moderate my expectations for what I think the world 'owes me'. I'll save up more gratitude for when special moments and kind people emerge. And you know what? Not only will I appreciate these fragile rare bits more gleefully when they occur, I will lay a bet that through my actions I attract more of them.

Yesterday, I had a good run of testing this out with success. I noticed plenty of triggers around me, walking the rainy streets of Dublin on Easter Sunday. I smiled at a grim neighborhood, because it didn't affect me. I apologized to a diagonal walker staggering and blocking my path, as I patiently waited then passed. I cheered 'Happy Easter' to a grimaced old man blowing vape mist in front of me, because he looked like he needed some cheer. I chuckled a little at his confused expression as I bounced along out of his life. I protected my calm with forgiveness over contempt. I can't promise or foresee how this tactic will grow, and I'm sure I'll need more tools to keep it intact. Many feelings in this life like happiness are fleeting and that's OK. It makes them beautiful, it gives them grace. But my calm is my totem, something to protect and dote on.

233

And my peace of mind is my gardenhouse to foster, more than a feeling, it might just be the powercell of the identity I desire.

ABOUT THE AUTHOR

Paul Carreo is an American born, Irish naturalised, speculative fiction writer. He has spent the past ten years writing fantasy fables and observational fiction. He is the founder of PC Studios, a publishing and media company. Paul has also worked over twenty five years in major technology companies, like Google, where he developed a persuasive sales & marketing voice, a passion for creative expression, and an eye for the delicious absurdity in all things stranger than fiction.

www.paulcarreo.com

Made in the USA
Las Vegas, NV
24 January 2024

84837271R10134